# "YOU'RE A DISGRACE TO THE CORPS!"

Hanlon cringed at the Admiral's icy stare.

"You had a good record, Hanlon—a fine future in the Interstellar Corps. Now you've thrown it away. There's no room in the Corps for a cheat!"

Hanlon blustered, "I didn't—you have no right—"

"That'll do!" Disgust showed on the Admiral's face as he gestured to the Marines, who grabbed Hanlon's arms and handcuffed him.

"George Hanlon, you are hereby dismissed from the Interstellar Corps' Cadet School!" And the Admiral ripped the identifying symbols from Hanlon's uniform. "Take him out of my sight!"

They hauled Hanlon away, disgraced. . . .

But inside, he was jubilant. Now his real job of counter-intelligence would begin!

# MAN
# OF MANY
# MINDS

## by E. EVERETT EVANS

PYRAMID BOOKS, New York

*To Thelma,*
*a wedding anniversary present*

MAN OF MANY MINDS

A PYRAMID BOOK
Published by arrangement with Fantasy Press

Pyramid edition published November, 1959
   Second printing, October 1968

PYRAMID BOOKS are published by Pyramid Publications, Inc.
444 Madison Avenue, New York, New York 10022, U.S.A.

# Chapter 1

CADET GEORGE HANLON STOOD STIFFLY AT attention. But as the long, long minutes dragged on and on, he found his hands, his spine and his forehead cold with the sweat of fear. He tried manfully to keep his eyes fixed steadily on that emotionless face before him, but found it almost impossible to do so.

Tension grew and grew and grew in the room until it seemed the very walls must bulge, or the windows burst to relieve the pressure. The cadet felt he could not stand another minute of it without screaming. Why didn't that monster say something? What kind of torture was this, anyway? And why was he here in the first place? He couldn't think of a single reg he had broken—yet why else would he be called before Admiral Rogers, the dread Commandant of Cadets?

In spite of his utmost efforts to stand eye to eye with the commandant, Hanlon couldn't keep his gaze steadily on that feared visage. His eyes insisted on straying, time after time, although he always forced them back. He caught glimpses of the dozens of communicator studs and plates on the huge metal desk. He saw the bit of scenery showing through the window. He noted the pictures of great Corps heroes that adorned the walls. In fact, he had to look at anything except those boring, impassive eyes fixed so steadily on his own face. If only he could gain such perfect control of his nerves. If only he knew what this was all about!

By the big wall chronom he saw he had already been standing there at rigid attention a full five minutes. The second hand crept around again. Six minutes! It dragged slowly around once again. Seven minutes.

Then the unbearable silence was mercifully broken by the admiral's voice.

"In some ways, Mister, you're quite a stupid young man," he said. "I'm inclined to be disappointed in you."

Hanlon gave a start of surprise, and forced himself to scrutinize more carefully that enigmatic face.

"What . . . what do you mean, sir?"

The stern eyes were still boring into his. But now the cadet thought he could detect a trace of secret amusement behind them.

"Why do you torture yourself like this? You know how to find out what it's all about."

There was a sinking feeling in George Hanlon's mind. Did that mean what he was afraid it meant?

He sent out a tentative feeler of thought toward the mind behind that expressionless face. He expected to find it difficult to do, because of long disuse of the faculty. But he was amazed both at the ease with which the technique returned to him, and with the feeling of warm friendliness he found in that mind—almost like a sort of fatherly pride.

He probed a bit deeper, and was aware of assurance that he had done nothing to merit punishment. Indeed, it seemed he could catch exactly the opposite feeling.

He must have shown his relief, for the commandant's stern face relaxed into a broad smile, and he lounged back in his big chair.

"That's better. At ease, and sit down."

Slowly, disbelieving the sudden change, the astonished young cadet gingerly sank onto the front edge of a chair. He had to, his legs were suddenly rubbery.

"I . . . I don't understand at all, sir."

The admiral leaned forward and spoke impressively. "Do you think, Cadet Hanlon, that we would let any man get to within weeks of graduation without knowing all about him?"

The young man's eyes widened, and his hands clutched at his knees in an effort to keep them from shaking.

"Oh, yes, we know all about you, George Spencer Newton Hanlon," and the cadet's eyes opened even wider at that name. "We know about your talent for mind-reading as a child, and how you suppressed it as you grew older

and found how it got you into trouble. We know all about
your father's disgrace and disappearance; your mother's
death; your running away, and your adoption by the
Hanlons, whose last name you assumed."

"How . . . how'd you learn all that, sir?"

"The Corps has its ways. And that's why you're here
now. Oh, all the Fifth Year Cadets will be interviewed
by myself or my assistants this coming week, to determine
their first assignment after graduation. But I called you
in today for a very, very special reason. And your ability
to read minds is part of it."

The cadet drew himself up stiffly. "I'm through with
all that, sir, definitely!"

The commandant regarded him enigmatically for a moment. "Just what do you expect to do in the Corps,
Mister?"

"Why, whatever I'm assigned to do, I suppose, sir. Or
whatever I can do."

"And just how far will you go for the Corps?" The
admiral leaned forward and eyed him critically.

"All the way, sir, of course."

"Don't you believe a Corpsman should use all his abilities in his service?" The question was barked at him.

"Certainly, sir." But his eyes showed he realized he
had been trapped by that admission.

"You're one of the few persons known who have ever
actually been able to read another's mind. That's important—very important—to the Corps. *It must be used!*"

Hanlon's eyes were still stormy, but he kept his lips
tightly closed.

The commandant's face grew kindly again. "We know
how it got you into trouble when you were a boy, because
the other children resented it, and avoided or abused you
for using it on them. But now it will be a great assistance
to you—and to the Corps. We know you will use that
talent wisely, for it has been proven time and again, by
test after test, that you are scrupulously honest. You've
lost your allowance several times in card games, when you
could have read what cards your opponents held, and so
won. You have let yourself fail on examination questions
you did not know, when you could have read the answers
in your instructor's mind."

"No, not that, sir," Hanlon shook his head. "I never could read from a mind such specific information as answers to questions or to problems."

"I imagine that will come when you start using your talent maturely," Admiral Rogers shrugged indifferently. "But at the moment I want to talk very seriously about your assignment. First, however, I must have your most solemn oath never to reveal what I am about to tell you, for it is our most carefully-guarded secret."

"I swear by my mother's memory, sir, never to reveal anything I am told to keep confidential."

"Very well. I have been delegated by the High Command to ask you to join the Secret Service of the Interstellar Corps."

Cadet George Hanlon drew in a sharp, startled breath and half-rose from his chair. "The . . . the Secret Service, sir? I didn't know there was one."

"I told you it was top secret," Admiral Rogers said impressively "We believe no one knows anything about its existence outside of the membership of that service, and officers of the rank of Rear Admiral or above."

The young cadet sat silent, his eyes on the tips of his polished boots, as though to see reflected there the answer to this astounding new situation that had been slapped into his consciousness.

This was all so utterly unforeseen. He had dreamed of doing great deeds in the Corps, of course, but actually had never expected to be assigned to anything but routine work at first. His mind was a chaotic whirlpool of conjectures. How could he fit into such an organization? Why had he been selected? Surely, the fact that as a child he was supposed to have been a mind-reader wasn't enough . . . or was it, from their standpoint?

After some time he looked up. "I don't know as I'd make a very good detective, sir."

Admiral Rogers threw back his head and laughed, breaking the tension. "I think, and so do the top men of the Secret Service, who have studied you thoroughly, that you will soon become one of its most useful members."

That was another shock, but out of it grew determination.

"Very well, sir, I'll try it."

"Good! But not 'try it,' Hanlon. Once you're in, it's for life. And there's one other thing I haven't told you yet. I couldn't, until after you had agreed to join. This may make you change your mind, which you are still at liberty to do."

The cadet's throat tightened, and he moistened his lips as he saw the admiral's face grow ominous.

"I want you to consider this very seriously," he said slowly, grimly, and Hanlon's probing mind caught the aura of importance in his manner. "Take your time, and figure carefully all the angles and connotations inherent in it, for it will not be an easy decision to make."

He paused impressively. "Here it is, cold! You'll have to be, apparently, dismissed from the Corps in disgrace. That is horribly harsh, we know," he added quickly, compassionately, as he saw the look of dismay that whitened the cadet's face. "But we have found over the years that it is the best way to make members of the SS most valuable to us. Every one of them has gone through the same thing, if that is any encouragement or consolation."

Young Hanlon's spirits sank to absolute nadir. "Not . . . not even graduate?" he whispered, agonizedly.

"Not publicly, with your class, no. But you'll be given private graduation, for you'll still be a member of the Corps."

He was silent again to allow the young man to recover a bit, then continued in a fatherly voice. "We know it's a terrible price to ask any man to pay. It takes guts to withstand, publicly and willingly, the dishonor, the loss of friends and the good will of people who know you. It means life-long disgrace in the eyes of the public and those members of the Corps who have ever known you or will hear of you."

The blood drained from Hanlon's face, his breathing was quick and rasping. The admiral's heart went out to him in sympathy, but he had to keep on. Now, though, he tried to soften the blow.

"Yet there are rewards in honor from those who do know. There will come a deep satisfaction from the years of devoting your life and abilities to the tremendous service of maintaining peace and security for all mankind of the entire Federation of Planets. Actually, the SS does more to keep that peace than all the rest of the Corps. So these things are, in the estimation of those who have gone through it, well worth any pain and humiliation they have to suffer."

His tone was so kind that Hanlon found a measure of comfort in the looks and attitude of the officer before him, now suddenly not a dread ogre, and martinet, but a kindly, fatherly, understanding friend.

George Hanlon sat with downcast eyes, thinking swiftly but more cogently than he had ever done before. He had come into this room still a boy despite his twenty-two years. Now, abruptly, he was roughly forced into manhood.

As such an adult, then, he quickly realized this was the crucial point in his life to date—probably in all the years to come. But to lose the respect and friendship of everyone he knew—he shuddered. To be despised, an outcast!

Yet Admiral Rogers said all the SS men had gone through it, and now felt it worth all the pain and disgrace, to be able to do the work they were doing.

He had been trained all his life, and especially in Corps school, to scan all available data for and against each problem that arose, and then make a decision quickly and intelligently.

He rose to his feet and straightened determinedly. "I'll still take it on, sir, if you and the general staff think I'm worthy and will be useful."

The admiral rose swiftly and came around the desk to grasp the cadet's hands in both of his. "I'm proud of you, my boy. It took real strength of character to make that decision. I'm sure you will never regret it, though there'll be moments when it will hurt to the pit of your soul, especially the first few days."

The cadet's eyes clouded again, and he shivered convulsively. "That part's got me in a blue funk, no fooling. Do you suppose I can take it, and not give the show away?"

Again the commandant's hearty, friendly laugh boomed out, filling the office with merriment and honest pride. "By Snyder, you will, Son, like a thoroughbred!" He went back behind that great desk, and was suddenly once more the strict disciplinarian. "Cadet Hanlon, 'ten-shun!" he barked.

The young man stood rigid.

"Raise your right hand. Do you swear before the Infinite Essence to uphold, with all your abilities, the Inter-Stellar Corps, and the laws and decisions of the Federated Planets?"

"On my honor, sir, and with God's help, I pledge allegiance to the Inter-Stellar Corps and to the people and governments of all the Federated Planets!"

Hanlon came to a punctilious salute, which Admiral Rogers returned as precisely before resuming his seat.

"Senior Lieutenant George Hanlon, at ease."

He grinned companionably at the young man's start of surprise. "Promotions are swift in the Secret Service, Hanlon. Now, go through that door. There you'll meet your immediate superior officer, who will give you instructions. And Hanlon, my sincerest personal good wishes. Safe flights, Lieutenant."

"Thank you, sir, for everything."

# Chapter 2

SENIOR LIEUTENANT GEORGE HANLON OPENED the designated door and stepped through into the next office. A grey-haired man, wearing the Twin Comets of a Regional Admiral, was sitting behind a desk, studying some papers. He continued sitting thus, the papers held so they hid his face, apparently so intent on his work he had not noticed anyone entering.

But Hanlon instinctively knew better, and stood stiffly at attention, awaiting the other's pleasure. Soon the man lowered the papers . . . and Hanlon gasped.

"Da . . .". His mouth snapped shut, and his eyes became

swiftly hostile at remembrance of the hate he had carried
all these years on account of this man. He wanted to stalk
out, but ingrained discipline chained him to the spot. His
voice, though, was very cold when he spoke. "Senior Lieutenant George Hanlon reporting, sir."

The big man was a startling older edition of the newly-
appointed lieutenant, only grey where the latter was blond,
assured from long, bitter experience where the other was
as yet untried. Now he rose to his feet, acknowledging
the salute.

"At ease. I can imagine your surprise at seeing me," and
if there was a hurt look on his face at sight of that im-
placable hatred in his son's eyes and demeanor, he could
not be blamed. "However, I think your experience of the
past hour might have prepared you for sight of me in
uniform. Yes," as he saw the sudden surprise in the
young man's eyes, "that was the reason for my apparent
disgrace. I hope you will forgive me, now that you know
why it was necessary."

"Of course," stiffly punctilious, "only," his eyes were
still hard and stormy, "was it important enough to break
mother's heart?"

The older man's voice grew soft and shook with genuine
emotion. "You and everyone had to believe that, Spence,
all these years. I've been prayerfully waiting for the day
when I could explain to you. I can assure you, Son," with
all the sincerity his voice could carry, "that she did not
die of a broken . . ."

"I know bet . . .".

"You do not know better!" his father interrupted
sternly. "Please wait until I finish explaining. No, Spence,"
his voice was still emphatic but softer now, almost pleading. "She knew and approved. Your mother was one of
Earth's greatest heroines."

Hanlon was still standing stiffly, but now his eyes
clouded with mixed emotions, of which doubt predomi-
nated. His mind touched that of his father, and he seemed
to read truth there. But could he believe this now . . .
after all those dreadful years?

"Actually," his father was continuing, "your mother
had become a victim of multiple sclerosis. When we knew
she had less than two months to live, I talked to her, with

the Corps' permission, about my going into Secret Service work. With her death so near, it could be done convincingly. Believing you would understand some day, and approve, she agreed. I'm terribly sorry for all you've had to suffer during the intervening years. Again I beg for giveness."

As his father talked, Hanlon's eyes and heart gradually lost their hardness, and at the end he ran forward and grasped the other's hands.

"Oh, Dad, I'm so sorry. I've hated hating you. If it hadn't been for the long talks Pa and Ma Hanlon had with me, I don't believe I would ever have gone into the cadet school."

The older man hugged his son hungrily.

"Believe me, Spence, it wasn't easy for me, either. But I didn't actually desert you, even though it had to seem so. I know everywhere you've been, everything you've done. You've been watched over constantly. I engineered your adoption by the Hanlons—he was a retired Corpsman, you know—and I've paid your expenses. You see, I happen to love my son very much."

"And I loved my Dad so, too. That's why it hurt . . . say, now I can change my name back, can't I? The Hanlons both died since I started cadet school, you know"

"Well . . . no, for the time being I think not. You're well known as 'Hanlon' now, and you'd better leave it that way, for now, at least. However, you'll find need of an alias from time to time in this new job—you can use it then. I certainly will be proud to have you wearing my name again."

But both men were shying away from all this frank expression of their emotion, and Hanlon dropped back a pace.

"How does it happen I've never seen you around the buildings or grounds here?"

"No one ever sees me in uniform, except in this or some other Base office on special occasions. Outside, I'm always disguised. When I come into a Reservation I'm a bearded janitor or something. You'll soon learn about disguising, yourself."

Then he became all business, and his face sobered as he went back to his desk.

"Sit there, Lieutenant. There's a lot to tell you, and you are to pay strict attention and get it all in this one interview, for there can't be another at this time. It would attract too much attention for you to be called here more than this once."

He smiled again, with a warm, fatherly pride. "First, let me congratulate you, officially on your decision, and to welcome you sincerely into the Secret Service."

Hanlon bowed in acknowledgement, then sat down and leaned forward attentively. "I'll try to get it all, sir."

"First, the matter of your dismissal. It will come some time within the next few days, but even I won't know ahead of time when or how it will happen. Some SS man unknown on Terra will be called in to attend to it. But when it does come you will recognize it almost instantly, and you must play it up big. Don't let on in any way that you suspect or know it is anything but genuine. You must impress on your fellow students, and upon everyone else you know or later come to know, that it was real, and that it has soured you for all time on the Corps, and on all law and order and government."

The young man nodded, but said nothing, for his throat was clogged and his spirits quailing at thought of that public disgrace. He had been so proud here . . . how could he possibly stand giving it all up? Maybe he was a fool ever to have agreed.

But the admiral was continuing. He shoved a sheaf of bills across the desk. "Here's a thousand credits. Use them to buy your civilian clothes and kit after your dismissal. Buy a few shares of some stock, too—the amount or value doesn't matter. Get a small insurance policy. Yes," seeing his son's questioning look, "there's a reason.

"After you get your clothing and things and have discarded your uniform, go rent a hotel room, then go to the Inter-Stellar bank and rent a safety deposit box. That's one of the first things you do in each city on any planet to which you may be sent on assignment. Now, here are two keys that fit box number 1044 in all the I-S banks. They are special master keys of our own designing. Box 1044 is used because of its nearness to those private booths, in the universal setup all I-S banks use. That box is our means of confidential communication.

"After you get into the vault ostensibly to get into your own box, use these to open box 1044. There's a little electronic gadget in each box 1044. When you want immediate service on anything you put into the box, press the red button on the mechanism. Go back a few hours later and it will have been attended to. So now, when you get into the bank, put a note there listing your hotel room number and also your new deposit key number. Come back in a couple of hours and you'll find a key that will have your box number stamped on it, but which will open both boxes. Then leave your old key and and one of these in 1044, and carry the other and the new one."

"Oh, I see. The stock and insurance policy in my own box are decoys, eh?"

"Right. You put all your reports in box 1044, and get your orders there. We all use 1044, so just sort through the envelopes for any with your name on them. The same key also locks the sound-proof and spyray-proof cubicle in the vault, so no one, not even another SS man, can interrupt you unless you want to let them in."

"My own box for decoy; 1044 for service matters; key fits both boxes and cubicles; red button for quick service. Yes, sir."

"When you get to a new city or planet, put your local address there as soon as feasible. That's your one sure contact. Also, in each box you'll find quite a lot of money at all times. You take what you need for expenses and get your salary that way. If your job calls for more than is in the box at any time, leave a request and press the red button. More will be brought immediately."

"That's quite a trust, sir," Hanlon gulped. "I hope I'll always use it wisely."

His father nodded and smiled. "You will, Spence. We wouldn't have asked you to join us if we weren't sure. As your father, I'm mighty proud to have you for a son. As Assistant Chief of the SS, I feel sure you'll be a credit to us.

"Now," all business again, "a sleep instructor and some reels of the language and other information about Simonides Four will be delivered to your hotel room. Simonides Four is your first assignment. There's something fishy going on there we haven't been able to find out about, but we think you can get us some good leads.

"Don't try to handle it alone—just get us information. And, son, use your talent for reading minds. I heard over the intercom all you said to Rogers, and while that wasn't the only reason you were asked into the SS, believe me, it will be tremendously important in your work with us— it'll help us where no other agent can get to first check station. And I have a feeling, too, that you'll develop both that and many other mental abilities once your mind starts to hit the ball. You'll find in this work every single talent and ability you can develop will be useful and needed."

"Yes," Hanlon nodded slowly, "I'm beginning to realize that. I'll practice a lot."

"As for money, don't be niggardly—spend what you like and always carry quite a bit with you for emergencies. Live well, although not extravagantly unless the occasion of your work demands it. Not to save money, but to remain as inconspicuous as possible."

"The Service has it all thought out, hasn't it?" Admiration shone in the young lieutenant's eyes.

"They've had a lot of years for it, Spence. Now, there's another means of contact, for cases of emergency. Get word to, or an interview with, any officer of the rank of Rear Admiral or above. The words 'Andromeda Seven' are the passwords to let him know who and what you are. Once you've made that contact, commandeer anything or any service needed to assist your work."

"I understand, sir." Hanlon strained to review all this new knowledge quickly. Then, "I'm sure I have it all. Get civilian kit; hotel room; stocks and insurance; deposit boxes—my own and 1044; sleep-learn Simonidean; 'Andromeda Seven'."

"Correct. Now, you'll be interested in a little of the background of the Secret Service. It was John Snyder himself who organized it, shortly after the formation of the Snyder Patrol. He realized almost at once that such an unknown, undercover echelon would be a must. There's usually not more than two hundred of us. New members are taken in only as replacements, or when some Corpsman with a special ability, such as your mind-reading, is discovered.

"We work anywhere throughout space when there's a

need, but there are usually one or two of us on each planet of the Federation at all times. When not on any special assignment we keep busy on some planet not our original home, checking the background of cadets or especially-appointed government workers, guarding VIP's, and such other vital matters. But whatever we are, or whatever we are doing, we are the Corps!

"We are mighty proud of the fact that no SS man has ever betrayed his trust, even to save his life. Our work is dangerous in the extreme, but without exception we are all men with high mental ability—quick-thinking, clever, and unusually adept at getting out of scrapes." He grimaced mirthlessly. "We learn that last mighty quick in this business . . . if we last.

"And to all of us, our dangerous, unadvertised, publicly unrecognized work is personally highly satisfying. We know we are the guardians of the peace of the Federation, even though we get no hero-worship from the populace who don't know we exist."

Hanlon nodded slowly, thoughtfully. "One thing puzzles me, Dad. You and Admiral Rogers both spoke about how secret all this is, yet I was given the chance to back out after I knew about it."

His father grinned. "Several have, over the years. They underwent treatment to erase that knowledge from their mind." He stood up and came around the desk to where his son had also risen. "I may not see you again before you leave, Spence . . . George, I mean," he smiled ruefully, then brightened. "But the best of luck, son, and keep in mind that you have the honor of the finest body of men in the Universe in your keeping, and always try to be worthy of the trust."

"I will, sir," gravely. "It seems almost too much responsibility for a cub like me, and I'm scared. But I'll do my best."

"Take it easy at first. Don't try too much, and don't put yourself in any more danger than you have to until you learn the ropes, which you will, faster than you may now think. On this assignment, all we ask is that you try to get us some leads we can work on."

"Right! I don't want to conk out too soon, now. I've got a lot of living I want to do first, especially now I've got my dad back again. I sure hope we manage to see each other fairly often."

"Oh, we undoubtedly will, except when one or the other of us is on a long job. We'll meet—somewhere— quite often."

"About this assignment of mine, Dad. Can you give me any dope on it?"

"You'll get what any of us know, from the reels, and the latest development from the box when you're ready to start out. Oh, yes, I almost forgot. The paper we use is a digestible plastic, so make a meal off all orders and confidential communications you receive. The box always contains a supply for your reports or requests for specific information or assistance."

"Saves money on feed bills, eh?"

His father grinned appreciatively, then sobered. "Make sure you understand each step you take first, and don't try to run until you know how to crawl. Well, safe flights, Spence."

"Safe flights to you, too, Dad, always. And I want you to know I'm so glad to have all those horrible misunderstandings and hates cleared away."

"I missed my boy, too. But 'vast rewards', you know."

With mixed sensations of high elation and worried fear, the swiftly-maturing young Corpsman walked slowly through the beautiful park that surrounded the great stainless-steel skyscraper that housed the cadets during their training period. His thoughts were as twisted as were the meandering paths and walks he trod so unseeingly.

# Chapter 3

As HANLON ENTERED HIS DORMITORY ROOM, his roommate looked up from his studies.

"What'd the Big Brass Bull want, Han?"

"Huh?" Hanlon snapped out of his abstraction and grinned. "Nothing important. You'll be up soon. Just about our first assignments after graduation." He was thinking swiftly. ". . . Uh, I get some extra instruction in piloting, and a chance at the controls."

"Gee, I hope they let me work on codes."

Hanlon shrugged. "They probably will, Dick. They try to fit us where we can do the most good, Rogers said." He picked up a book and sat down, apparently studying intently, and young Trowbridge resumed his own lessons.

Hanlon began practicing his mind-reading at every opportunity. At first he felt sure he would be caught at it, but quickly remembered that, as a child, his victims never suspected they were being mentally invaded unless he told them or acted carelessly upon information so gleaned.

Yet it had been his naive, boyish pride then, that had made him boast to his playmates of his ability, and prove it by telling them things he had learned about them. All that, naturally, got him into much trouble and not a few fights, and caused the loss of all his early boyhood friends. That was why he had quit using his wild talent and had been so determined never to do so again, as he had first told Admiral Rogers.

But now he realized he must use it with all the ability and skill he could acquire. For this mind-reading, whatever of it he could do, was decidedly his dish. The SS would be sure to hand him all the jobs where it might best get them what they needed—if he showed he could produce.

Yet with his present equipment Hanlon knew he could do little. As he had also told the commandant, he couldn't actually read anyone's mind to the extent of getting definite wording or specific information. But he could get quite clear sensory impressions that helped him deduce what the other person was thinking.

He had partially learned—and now practiced with all his abilities and gained knowledge and intellect to improve and perfect the technique—to gauge the other's looks, glances, facial expressions, muscle movements, sudden tensenesses, and so on. For those, together with the mood-impressions and bits of fleeting thoughts, enabled him to know almost to a certainty what the other was actually thinking at the observed time.

In the barracks, later that first evening, he got into a card game and concentrated on trying to win by this method. Nor was it consciously that he chose a game being played for low stakes—he just wouldn't have thought of trying to win large sums by such "cheating".

For some time he won consistently and easily. He couldn't know what cards his opponents held, by suit or number, but he could tell without any difficulty whether each of the other players felt he had a poor, medium or good hand. By playing his own accordingly, his wins were far greater than his losses. After an hour or so of play had proved he could do it, and had given him considerable practice, Hanlon closed his mind to their impressions. He now played his cards so recklessly he soon lost his winnings. Then he got out of the game on a plea of having to study.

The next morning during first class, the door opened and Admiral Rogers entered the classroom.

" 'Ten-shun!" the teacher called, springing to his feet.

"As you were. I want to borrow one of your young gentlemen for the day, Major. A VIP is in town, and we want to give him an aide." He looked about the room, as though to pick out a likely-looking candidate. "How about Cadet Hanlon? Does he especially need today's lesson?"

"Oh, no, sir, he's one of our top students."

Admiral Rogers looked directly at Hanlon, who had risen to attention when his name was mentioned. "In my office, in full dress uniform, on the double."

"Dismiss, Hanlon," the instructor said, and the cadet ran out.

In Admiral Rogers' office ten minutes later, Hanlon received his instructions. "Report to the Simonidean Embassy and put yourself at the disposal of Hector Abrams, First Secretary to the Simonidean Prime Minister. But first, hang this stuff on you. This dress sword is a little unusual—the scabbard is rounder than yours, but not noticeably so. It's really a blaster; the trigger is here on the handle as you grasp it. Put on these aide's aguillettes —the metal tips are police whistles. No," seeing Hanlon's questioning look, "we don't expect any trouble today—

these are just routine, for we like to be ready for emergencies."

Hanlon fastened the braided cords to his shoulder tabs, and belted on the twenty-inch-long blaster-sword. The admiral touched a switch on his desk and spoke into a microphone. "My personal car to take Cadet Hanlon to the Simonidean Embassy, then return."

At the Embassy, Hanlon reported to the receptionist, and was shown with due deference into one of the private offices, where he was introduced to several men, among them the Secretary he was to accompany.

"I have a number of errands to do today, but the first and most important is laying the cornerstone of our new Embassy building—this one is merely rented, you may know."

"I am entirely at your disposal, sir," Hanlon saluted crisply, and fell into step just behind the portly statesman as he left the building.

They rode in an open car with a uniformed chauffer, the others following in other cars. As they rode Hanlon probed the statesman's mind, but found only worry-tension, that he shrewdly guessed had to do with the coming speech, rather than with any thought of intrigue or illegal machination.

As they came into the Greek section of the city, their ride took on more and more the aspects of a parade, as the Simonidean was recognized.

Hanlon opened his mind wide and attempted to analyze the thought-sensations he received from the crowds. It was one of gaiety and good nature, and reminded him of the way his boyish mind interpreted the thoughts of holiday crowds at the circus, Fourth of July celebrations, picnics, and so on.

From the moment he first entered the Embassy, Hanlon had been probing with every iota of his ability, hoping he could find some lead to whatever it was that was bothering the Corps about Simonides, but had found nothing sinister or menacing, nor could he get any such sensations from the crowd.

But now he concentrated more on watching the increasingly denser throng of people, for the car was nearing their destination. The buildings along here were all bedecked with Simonidean and Greek-Terran flags, and there was now a continuous cheering from the populace. Abrams was standing in the back of the car now, smilingly acknowledging their plaudits by bowing to one side and the other.

Hanlon, sitting stiffly at attention, nevertheless kept his eyes darting here and there, watching as carefully as he could for any possible hostile demonstrations or menacing figures.

Arrived at the building site, Abrams was greeted by numerous dignitaries, and escorted with much pomp to the flag-bedecked stand, amid greater cheering from the assembled crowd.

The chairman of the occasion stepped to the public-address microphone, and raised his hands for silence. The band broke off in the middle of a number, the cheering from the huge throng gradually died down, and the ceremony got under way.

Hanlon, who had taken his post at one corner of the platform, paid scant attention to what was happening on it, as it neither interested him nor could he understand too much of it, even though he knew quite a bit of Greek. Again his eyes were busy continually looking all about the great crowd and the surroundings.

Nothing of note occurred until the chairman began introducing Abrams, and then hecklers in the crowd began shouting:

"Freedom for the Greeks of Simonides!"

"Empires are out of date; let the people rule!"

"Demos forever!"

These calls were few at first, but the men yelling them were leather-lunged. The chairman's face turned reddish, and he wavered a bit in his speech, then raised his own voice in an attempt to drown out the interruptions.

Others were now crying out, though still only a few, but in spite of their shouts the ceremonies continued, and Abrams, properly introduced, rose and began his prepared speech.

Hanlon, more alert than ever, could see local police shoving through the crowd, trying to apprehend and silence the hecklers. But from his vantage point Hanlon saw the latter shifting rapidly from place to place, partly to escape detection, he swiftly deduced, and partly to make it seem as though more and more people were joining in the demonstration.

In a side glance Hanlon saw that the Secretary was nettled at the disturbance, and his color was high although he bravely continued speaking. The great audience was largely paying attention to him, and must have found him interesting, from their frequent cheers.

Suddenly, at one side, there seemed to be a more determined demonstration, and Hanlon tore his gaze from it, remembering his instructor's words:

"Disregard specific diversions in one spot! Let the police handle those—you must watch most carefully then for assassins!"

Instantly he was more alert, more carefully scanning the whole scene before him, his eyes travelling forth and back.

A glint of reflected sunlight from a nearby roof jerked his eyes upward, and at what he saw, with one swift, smooth motion he drew his blaster-sword, sighted carefully, and pressed the trigger.

There was a crack of flame, and a gunman half-hidden behind a chimney screamed, half-rose, then, his body charred by the force of that blast, toppled from the roof into the street below, his rifle falling near him. Hanlon swivelled. "Cover Abrams!" his voice rang out commandingly, and he himself jumped in front of the Secretary while others on the platform sprang up to completely surround the Simonidean, and hide him from possible further danger.

Hanlon raised one of the tassel-whistles and blew a piercing blast. Now he could see several local policemen running toward the platform, and in moments Abrams, surrounded by an armed and alert escort, was hustled into a waiting police car, which sped back to the Embassy.

The Simonidean was white and shaking, upset by the episode.

"Why?" he kept asking, but no one had any answers. "I'm not important enough for anyone to want to kill," Abrams shook his head. "The people of Simonides like the empire status—why should anyone here on Terra object?"

"There's always crackpots in every crowd," a police

captain said. "We get riots like this one almost every time there's a public ceremony. Most of 'em're plain nuts —once in a while only is there one who feels he's got a real grievance, personal."

"But with so many participating, this one looked planned," Hanlon objected. "I was higher and watching, and I could see at least a dozen men shouting at the beginning, starting all at the same time, although a lot more took it up. It must have been a plot of some kind."

His mind was racing. Was this part of what he was being sent to Simonides to investigate? He had tried to probe the crowd minds, but there were so many conflicting thought-emanations, such a welter of sensations he wasn't able to isolate any single, individual moods or thoughts.

Safely back inside the Embassy, Abrams seemed to relax a bit. He turned now to Hanlon.

"My very sincere thanks, young man, for your quickness and alertness in saving my life. I shall be eternally grateful."

Hanlon waved his hand deprecatingly. "It was my job, sir. I'm sorry your day was spoiled that way."

"I still can't make out why?" The Simonidean said slowly, and Hanlon, probing, could sense that his mind was full of question marks. "I'm not that important. If it had been the emperor"—Hanlon caught an impression of loyalty and love for that dignitary—"or even the Minister"—here he caught a feeling of doubt and some dislike—"it might make sense. Just as I cannot figure out why I should have been sent here for this purpose. It's almost . . ." he was silent, and Hanlon's probes found only puzzlement.

"Nuts!" the young Corpsman felt frustrated. "If only I could really read minds! I think this guy knows something I want to learn, but I can't get the least idea of what it is."

But he kept trying, and not only with the mind of this one man he had been sent here to guard. He reached out to all other minds in the room, but none of them seemed to have any thoughts about the why of this unexpected happenstance. There were mostly feelings of anger that their beautiful new Embassy building had not been properly dedicated, and their ceremony ruined.

Abrams had sunk into a chair, and it soon became apparent to Hanlon that he wasn't planning on handling any of his other outside errands that day.

"Will you want me any more, sir?" he finally asked after a considerable period of uneasy fidgetting. The Simonidean broke out of his abstraction, and rose to his feet.

"No, I shall stay here for the balance of the day at least. You may as well return to your other duties. Again, thank you, personally, for saving my life, and please express my thanks to the Corps for sending you. But I still can't understand . . ." He turned away, muttering.

Hanlon saluted the other members of the Embassy staff, and rode the slideways back to Base, reporting to Admiral Rogers, to whom he gave a full and concise account of all that had happened.

"Whatever Mr. Abrams and the police may think, I still believe it was all carefully planned," he concluded thoughtfully. "It wasn't just one man, for I could see at least a dozen. Though, of course," he added quickly, "one man may have been behind it."

"Undoubtedly," the admiral said. "There was the chance of something like this, which is why I picked you for the job, hoping you could get some leads from it."

"I told you I couldn't read specific thoughts or information," Hanlon said. "If you and the top brass picked me for the SS because you thought I could, you'd better release me from it. I can't work in a crowd at all, for there's such a jumble of thought-emanations I can't separate them. Even working with an individual I can only sense something of his feelings. Just as now," he grinned mirthlessly, "you're disappointed because I didn't get any data, and thinking my so-called mind-reading is all a fake."

The admiral almost jumped. "Why, I am not . . . ," then he looked surprised, and laughed. "By Snyder, I was, too!" He sobered. "But if you can do that, even if you can't actually read the words of the thought, you'll still be able to help, I'm sure. No, you keep on studying. I'll bet you'll be able to do a lot more before long."

"I sure hope so," Hanlon slowly unfastened the aiguellettes and removed the sword and belt, laying them on the corner of the big desk. At touch of that weapon he suddenly realized what he had done with it, and shuddered, while his face grew white and strained.

"What's the matter?" the admiral asked anxiously.

"I . . . killed . . . a . . . man," Hanlon trembled.

"No! You killed a snake!" Admiral Rogers laid his arm comfortingly about the younger man's shoulders. "It isn't the same at all. Don't let it bother you."

Hanlon tried manfully to rise from his dark mood. "You're right, in a way, sir, and I'll try to look at it that way. As to the mind-reading, I'll keep on trying, and I hope I can prove of some use."

The admiral patted his shoulder encouragingly. "You will. Dismiss."

# Chapter 4

THE CADETS WERE ALL KEYED UP ABOUT graduation, now so near, and most of them were cramming at every opportunity on the subjects in which they felt themselves deficient. Such tenseness is natural before any final examinations, but in their case more so than it would have been in an ordinary school or university.

For not until the final marks were posted from these last examinations, plus their marks for the entire five years, would any of them—except Hanlon, of course—know for a surety that he would be graduated and become a permanent member of the Inter-Stellar Corps. And how intensely each of them wanted to belong!

Four days had now passed since George Hanlan's fateful interview with the Commandant of Cadets, and its unexpected outcome. He could hardly believe, even yet, that he was now actually a member of the unknown Secret Service of the Corps.

Only the great inner joy he knew at the recovery of his once-adored dad, and the complete dismissal of all those black hatreds, gave proof that it wasn't all a fantastic dream.

Hanlon hadn't experienced anything unusual in the cadet routine, and was growing more and more nervous as to just what was to happen to him. He still shivered every time he thought of that coming, dreaded ordeal. And all this waiting, this worrying, this wondering when—it wasn't making life any easier. If only they would get it over and done with!

But he strove to compose himself for it as best he could, and it was a measure of his inherent stability that he never let his comrades, even his roommate, see how apprehensive he was.

Now the day had come for the first of their finals. Hanlon never worried about exams, for he had always been near the top of his class. Now, especially, since he was already graduated and a Senior Lieutenant, he could have taken things easily. But pride in his scholarship made him anxious as always to do his best.

Their first examination was History, one of Hanlon's pet subjects, for he loved this story of Mankind, his ups and downs and gradual growth.

When the examination papers were handed out and he noted the first question he smiled. If only they were all that easy.

> "Give briefly a resume of the events leading up
> to the formation of the Inter-Stellar Corps."

Hanlon uncapped his writo, and began:

"In the middle of the Twentieth Century the various governments of Earth were all tending toward either a totalitarian or a welfare-form state. More and more power became vested in the Executive branch; more and more citizens were either working directly for government, or were supported by relief funds. Business was, to an increasingly greater extent, stifled by over-control. Public debts became a staggering load, and workers had less and less of their income available for living needs.

"When atomic energy was first released by the United

States, in the form of a bomb during a war, the military took complete control of it. Neither private nor industrial scientists or technicians were allowed to experiment with possibilities of getting power directly from atomic fission.

"In 1958 a young man named Travis Burkett was elected to the United States Congress from California. During his four terms as member of the Lower House he became increasingly well-known as possessor of one of the finest minds in public life. In 1966 he was advanced to the Senate, and soon became its leading member.

"In 1976 (prophetic year) he ran for President on the simple platform of 'give the country back to the people'. His ideas and views so fired the minds and hopes of the citizens of America, regimented and ground down by the cancerous growth of bureaucracy, that even most of the bureaucrats and reliefers joined to elect him by one of the greatest pluralities ever polled.

"During his two terms of office, with the help of a Cabinet of men who believed as he did, he fulfilled his promises. The tremendous power of the Executive was gradually returned to the Legislative, where it belonged. Unnecessary, over-lapping, and duplicated bureaus and agencies were reduced to the minimum. Only persons actually in need were supported from the public purse. Where almost 80% of the citizenry had been working for or supported by government when he took office, less than 15% were doing so when he retired.

"Tax restrictions and governmental meddling in industry and business were reduced save for a few necessary safeguards of minimum-wage and maximum-safety laws. With these restrictions removed, and with control of so many vital sciences and technologies taken away from the military, inventions took an accelerated up-swing.

"The peoples of other countries, fired by the realization of what could be done, staged revolutions, happily largely bloodless, and soon, working through the United Nations Council, a United World government became an actuality, and Burkett one of its first presidents.

"An American named John Snyder had, years before, secretly worked out a simple and inexpensive method of obtaining practically unlimited power directly from atomic fission. Now he could legally bring this to the public, and soon homes, public transportation and industry were using his power method.

"Snyder attracted to him a group of gifted scientists and technicians. These now turned their attention to space flight and Man, the Insatiable, began stretching out greedy hands to the Stars.

"They put a robot rocket on the Moon in less than two years. Their third rocket carried two scientists who did not make the return trip—they stayed to study and to learn. Five years later the first ship landed on Mars, and within a decade that planet was largely colonized. So, two years later, was Venus. Another fifteen years saw colonization of most of the moons of the outer planets.

"For, using new techniques and inventions learned from many experiments, the moons and planets were given air, water and warmth as needed. Android robots, developed by Varney, one of Snyder's scientists, helped greatly in this work, especially one young female android who was a true genius.

"Then Man reached the Stars . . . and the planets of those distant suns. It was here that the now-aged Snyder proved himself again one of the greatest humanitarians ever to have lived. He promulgated the ruling that is still in force:

"'Man must never colonize any planet having inhabitants intelligent enough to show cultural activity and growth'.

"Controlling all means of transportation between planets as he did, because he held all the basic patents, Snyder was able to enforce that ruling. To do so, he organized the 'Snyder Patrol', which later was taken over by the Federated Planets when that organization was formed, and became today's Inter-Stellar Corps.

"Today there are fifty-seven planets colonized by former inhabitants of Tellus or their descendants from colonized planets. These each have their own sovereignty and chosen form of government, but are united in a loosely-knit Federation which is solely a Court of Arbitration for Inter-Planetary affairs. The I-S C is the Federation's

Investigation and Enforcement branch, not a governing or military patrol."

Hanlon had finished that question and the second, which asked for the dates of the war between the colonists of Mars and those of the Jovian satellites. He was resting his eyes by glancing unseeingly about the room momentarily before starting the third question, when he heard the loud, angry voice of the instructor in charge.

"Cadet Hanlon, on your feet, sir! Just how, Mister, do you think you can get away with cheating at a final examination?"

Hanlon's head jerked up and his face went dead-white as the blood drained from it. He stumbled to his feet and, conscious of the amazed expressions of his classmates, looked up at the teacher.

"Bu . . . but I don't understand, sir. I wasn't cheating."

"Don't lie to me!" the voice was a whiplash. "I distinctly saw you looking at Cadet Fox's paper. The idea of any cadet, this close to graduation, trying such a contemptible thing!"

Hanlon's bewilderment was changing to anger at such an unjust accusation, when suddenly a thought struck him . . .

*This was it!*

Cheating at examinations always meant expulsion and disgrace.

He had all he could do to keep from betraying himself as he probed quickly toward the mind on the rostrum. Now he perceived the feeling of commiseration which the stern, hot eyes of the apparently outraged instructor did not reveal.

Hanlon remembered his father's instructions to "play it up big". He made himself glare back at the teacher, and his blue eyes took on the hardness of glacial ice.

"You're making a colossal mistake, sir," his voice was louder and angrier than it should ever have been. "If our regular instructor was giving this exam he'd never make such an accusation. I've led this class in grades all through school. And not by cheating, either."

"Lower your voice, Mister, and don't talk back!" But Hanlon's mind-probing was receiving approbation now. "I saw you cheating, and I know what I saw. Do you want to resign, or will you force me to take you to the commandant?"

"I don't know who you are, but you're a stupid fool!" Hanlon apparently lost all control of himself, and his voice and red face showed the anger he was simulating so well. "If you think you're going to frame me out of this class and out of graduating, you're a confounded idiot! Ask any of these chaps here—they all know I'm not a cheat."

But the cadets, though puzzled and dismayed, were far too clever to get mixed up in this unexpected brawl. They all sat, eyes lowered but faces straight ahead, arms folded across their chests, having no part in it at all.

The examining instructor, a man much larger and heavier than Hanlon's five feet eleven inches and one hundred and seventy-five pounds, rushed down from the platform. He grabbed at the cadet's arms, but Hanlon swivelled away, then stepped back in and struck at the officer.

That was mutiny! It was unthinkable for a cadet to strike an officer, under any circumstances or provocation.

The teacher, however, snared the cadet in a neo-judo hold that no neophyte, however skilled or strong could break. He dragged the struggling Hanlon up to the rostrum and, with his elbow, activated the intercom.

"Ask the commandant to come to room 12-B. A cadet, caught cheating at examinations, has mutinied."

Still holding the struggling, angry Hanlon, the instructor-officer excoriated his victim for such breach of cadet honor. Hanlon, meanwhile, yelled insults and oaths. He twisted and squirmed as though trying to escape, although he had quickly realized he was now being held in a loose though apparently-valid grip he could have broken easily had he so desired.

Yet during all this Hanlon was receiving from the officer's mind the distinct impression that the latter hated what he was doing, yet was approving the way the new SS man was playing his part. Further, Hanlon sensed he was being welcomed into the fellowship of those unknown SS men to whom he was now brother.

Soon Admiral Rogers, followed by two hulking space marines, came running into the room.

"What's going on here?" he barked.

Quickly the teacher repeated his charges, while Hanlon yelled denials and vituperations at the moronic imbecile who dared accuse him of such treachery.

"I'm ashamed of you, Hanlon!" the admiral said coldly. "We had high hopes for you, as I told you when I interviewed you about your initial assignment."

"Then why don't you listen to me instead of taking the word of this slime-snake who calls himself an instructor? Bah! He oughta be digging ditches!"

"That'll do!" Disgust showed on the admiral's face as he gestured to the marines, who jumped forward and grabbed Hanlon's arms, twisting them behind his back and handcuffing them.

"George Hanlon, you are hereby officially dismissed from the Inter-Stellar Corps' Cadet School!"

So saying, Admiral Rogers ripped all identifying symbols from Hanlon's uniform, then turned again to the marines. "Take him outside the Reservation."

They hauled Hanlon, still shrieking and cursing, out of the room, out of the building, across the park, and to the gate of the Corps' property.

There his handcuffs were removed, and the sneering marines literally and not-too-gently booted him into the street, where he sprawled face downward in a muddy puddle.

Hanlon pulled himself erect, apparently mad clear through. He shook his fist at the grinning marines gathered just inside the gate. He cursed them fluently with every foul oath and name he could remember ever having heard. Innately clean of speech and thought, this swearing nearly gagged him. But he was "putting on a good act."

They stood his insults for some time, but when he began to get too personal, a couple of them started toward him, their mocking laugher gone. To "make his act better," Hanlon now pretended to be frightened, cowardly, and accompanied by the jeers of the civilian on-lookers who had quickly congregated to see what all the rumpus was about, he fled down the city street away from the Reservation.

At first opportunity, after he had outdistanced his pursuers, Hanlon ducked into an alley. He ran down this until he spotted the back door of a little cafe, and dodged inside. There, in the washroom, he cleaned himself as best he could.

Again somewhat presentable, he left by the front door and rode the slideways to a section of the city where he could buy some good but not too expensive clothing.

Now inconspicuously dressed, he got a hotel room, then went to the bank where he bought some shares of stock, arranged for insurance, and rented a deposit box.

# Chapter 5

IN THE HOTEL ROOM ASSIGNED HIM, GEORGE Hanlon threw himself on the bed and for an hour lay there reviewing this sudden, strange turn of events, and all it presaged. He tried in vain to thrust out of his mind the astonished consternation of his classmates, the sneers of the marines and the jeers of the civilians there at the gate, who had seen his disgrace. Almost in tears now, he realized at last this was but a prelude to years of being scorned and vilified as a despised outcast.

Finally he calmed a bit, then got up to pace the room, wondering what the next move would be. The answer came almost at once. A rap on the door disclosed a messenger with a package for him. On opening it, after the man had gone, Hanlon found the sleep-instructor and reels. On top was a smaller reel marked, "No. 1. Listen to this awake."

He plugged in the machine, and put on the reel. It was his father's voice.

"You've got this far, now begins your real work. You should be able to memorize the contents of these reels in two weeks. Briefly, here is what they contain. Simonides Four was colonized under the direction of a Greek merchant who gave it his name. Four is the only habitable planet. Most of the original inhabitants under him were of his nationality, and the present language is an outgrowth of modern Greek, which you know somewhat. There are now, of course, many variations and new words, terms peculiar to their growing and evolving culture. The reels give all this more fully.

"The last reel tells their history, geography and economic situation as of today. Also, details about their various large cities, especially New Athens, their capitol. We believe you will find that city the best place to start your investigations. When you have these reels memorized, go to the bank, get your final instructions from the box, and your money for the trip.

"As to the problem, again briefly this is it: In the past year or so Federation agents have sensed a movement there, but have not been able to interpret it. Whatever it is, it is very, very secret—the agents can't even tell if it is political, religious, or merely social. Also, they have discovered that many important men, as well as dozens—maybe hundreds—of less important men, have mysteriously disappeared. All this has the smell of trouble for the Federation.

"At last the Secret Service was called in. We sent first one man, then a second. They tried to 'bore from within' by joining whatever the movement was. But they haven't been able to get even a start—they've hit it and bounced. The second is still there, still trying.

"As a matter of fact, we have no evidence at all, merely a sort of 'hunch', or presentiment, of a plot against the peace and welfare of the Federated Planets. There may be nothing wrong at all, but we don't like to take chances. With your ability to read minds you may be able to find out. We hope so."

Hanlon thought the message was ended, but then the voice began again. "I was told you came through your disgrace-scene very well. I know just what you are undoubtedly feeling at the moment, Spence—how sick at heart you are—and I only wish there was some way of easing your pain. But it will pass.

"Good luck, son, and safe flights. Take care of yourself. We're all behind you, and by the devious ways you know you can call on any or all of us at need. These reels are all water soluble, so dissolve them in the washbowl and flush down the drain as soon as you're through with each."

For the next two weeks Hanlon stayed fairly close to his room, studying by day from books obtained at the library the things he was learning at night via the sleep-instructor.

The evening of Graduation Day he sat miserably in front of a video screen in his room, watching the broadcast of the stately ceremony of which he would have been a part but for his decision to join the Secret Service.

All the longings of the years he had wanted to become a part of the Inter-Stellar Corps; all the hopes and plans he had made during his five long years in cadet school; all the thrilling pride he had known that he was to be a part of the greatest organization in the Universe, swelled inside him and choked him.

When, at long last, the class rose to take the Oath of Allegiance, Hanlon found himself on his feet, rigidly at attention, repeating the impressive ritual aloud with them.

Now, for the first time, despite his decision and his private graduation, he truly felt himself a vital part of the Corps.

On the street on his way to the library the following day, Hanlon chanced to meet a small group of his former classmates, now clad in their brand-new dress uniforms of sky-blue and crimson, their new junior lieutenant's bars shining brightly.

"Hi, fellows!" he greeted them, only to be met by silent glares of contempt.

"Aw, look, fellows, you know I was framed," Hanlon planted himself in front of them, and made himself look hurt, nor was that any effort. This really cut deep. But he had to "play it out"; had to make them keep on thinking his disgrace was real.

"You guys know I'd never do anything like that," he continued plaintively. "I didn't cheat—didn't need to. I know I lost my head when he accused me, but anyone'd do that."

"You mean you were never caught cheating before," Trowbridge sneered. "You sure had me . . . us . . . all

fooled. Now scram, or else . . . ." He doubled his fists
and took a step toward Hanlon.

The latter still played out his string, but his heart was
sick. He liked the fellows—they had been among his best
friends for five long, happy years. Only now was he truly
beginning to realize what a tremendous price he was
paying . . . and would have to pay all his life.

He stepped in and swung . . . and was instantly the
target for flying fists. He was knocked down several times,
but always managed to get up again. He had been well
trained in fighting of all types—and now he was putting
all his knowledge and skill into use—but only for defense
and the pretense of attack.

Even so he was getting badly mauled, for they were as
well trained—and were five to his one. His clothes were
dirty and ripped from the knock-downs, and a button was
torn off his coat. His knuckles were skinned, and he could
feel that his face was becoming a mass of bruises. A hard
left connected with his mouth, and he spat out a broken
tooth.

" 'Ten-shun!" a commanding voice suddenly broke in.

Instantly the five Corpsmen jumped back and, so ingrained was the training he had received, so did Hanlon,
to come at salute as they saw a High Admiral climbing
out of a ground-cab at the curb.

Hanlon, instantly realizing he wasn't in uniform and
was supposedly a discharged Corpsman, quickly dropped
his salute and slouched truculently.

"What's going on here!" the officer asked icily.

"This man's a disgraced cadet, sir. Cheated on final
exams," one of them explained. "He tried to talk to us."

"It's a lousy lie!" Hanlon rasped. "I was framed. The
Corps. Paugh!" he spat in pretend disgust. "I'm getting
out of here just as damned quick as I can, and as far as
I can. I'll go clear to Andromeda Seven if I can raise
enough credits!"

Only he, apparently saw the minute widening of the
admiral's eyes at that code-word. The officer faced the
new lieutenants sternly.

"A Corpsman is supposed to be able to handle five
civilians, not five Corpsmen to one. If this man is a disgraced cadet, you have a right to feel as you do about him.

But leave him alone—the years will bring him more sorrow and pain than you can with your fists. And you, fellow," turning to Hanlon. "Don't think I'm interfering just to save your worthless skin," his tone was one of utmost contempt. "I just don't want Corpsmen fighting on the street. Dismiss."

The five saluted smartly and marched away. The admiral winked briefly and with respect at Hanlon before reentering his cab.

But as the young man hurried back to his hotel to clean up, he was heartsick, remembering the many, many months of pleasant companionship with those boys. Especially Dick Trowbridge, who had been his roommate and special chum all through cadet school, and who today had seemed particularly disgusted and vicious in that fight.

Giving up all that had made life so happy and wonderful was more than a fellow could bear, his bitter thoughts ran. What a fool he had been to let himself be talked into taking this on. Where were all those "vast rewards" his dad and Admiral Rogers had talked about so eloquently? How could anything possibly make up for losing the respect and friendship of everyone he had ever known?

However, he had to admit, though still doubtfully, Dad had gone through it even to the point of giving up his son, and those last few weeks with his adored wife, yet now seemed satisfied and content. Maybe . . . maybe there was something behind it all, that time would prove. But it was mighty hard to take, just the same.

And this throbbing toothache didn't help his feelings any, either. The exposed nerve in that broken tooth made it ache like blazes. He'd better get it fixed before it drove him mad.

He started to go out, then stopped with the realization he had no money of his own to pay a dentist for the extraction and a bridge.

"What do I do in a case like this?" he wondered. "Is it ethical in such a purely personal matter, to use Corps funds? Dad didn't mention things of this sort. On the other hand, he said we got our salaries and expenses that way. Besides, you could say I lost the tooth in line of duty, and the Corps should replace it."

He went on, found a dentist and had the work done. Nor did he ever again feel doubt about spending the Corps' money for things he actually needed . . . but neither did he ever spend any on purely personal pleasures or extra comforts save as he needed to do so to play up to whatever position he assumed in the prosecution of his various assignments.

Evening, however, found him still with that smothered feeling of self-pity about his fight with the fellows, and it persisted even after he went to bed. By the Shade of Snyder, it wasn't fair to saddle a thing like this on a mere kid.

It wasn't until after a couple of hours of tossing sleeplessness that he remembered he hadn't turned on the sleep-instructor. Half-rebelliously, he nevertheless got up and did so . . . and that little act broke his mood. He dropped asleep almost immediately after returning to bed.

At the end of the two weeks Hanlon felt he knew both the Simonidean language and its customs well enough to start working. He went to the bank and, deviously, to box 1044.

Sorting through a thick sheaf of envelopes he found one with his name on it. He took it to one of the cubicles, whose door he locked from the inside, setting up full coverage.

As he read there flashed through his mind the background of this other planet's situation. From his knowledge of politico-history within the Federation he knew there was an iron-clad agreement that each planet could choose its own form of government. Most of them chose the democratic form, but some had a type of fascistic state. One or two—the most advanced—even had an anarchistic state, with a very minimum of laws and governing.

Simonides had, about a century earlier, reverted to the empire status—the only planet within the Federation to do so. It had originally been colonizd as a world-wide republic, but later had broken up into five independent countries, as different sections became populated more heavily with people of other national backgrounds than

Greek. These five countries had eventually been recombined, after a spectacular coup, as an empire.

Then had come this belief of the Corps that something was brewing there that would affect the peace of the Federation, and the failure of their agents so far to find out about it.

Now SSM Hanlon's orders were to take ship to Simonides Four, and seek to learn what he could about these guessed-at conditions as swiftly as possible. If he gained any impressions of who or what group was behind this movement, he was to attempt to join it and ferret out that secret so it could be reported.

With such information in their possession, the Corps would know if it was anything inimical to the peace and security of the Federation, and would take the necessary steps.

His instructions ended, "The cost of a first class ticket to Simonides is seven hundred and fifty credits, so you should draw enough to have at least fifteen hundred, for all needed expenses. Take the 'Hellene' which leaves Centropolis spaceport Friday of this week. We have good reason to believe that certain interesting people will be aboard that ship."

Hanlon's mind raced. Evidently someone wanted him to see what impressions or evidence he could pick up from those suspected persons. He grimaced as he realized the SS had left it strictly up to him to discover who those "interesting people" were. Perhaps they looked on it as a sort of test.

But he thrilled to the sudden awareness of what a wonderfully efficient and competent organization the SS was—how it kept careful watch on all its members, and assisted them in every possible manner.

He "dined" on the edible plastic sheets, then left the safety deposit vault. He arranged for his ticket and reservations at the bank's travel agency, then went back to his hotel to pack.

# Chapter 6

So it was that early Friday morning George Hanlon, still dressed in civvies, of course, arrived at the great passenger liner that was to take him to far Simonides. He was thrilled with the idea of making such a trip, for he loved the deeps of space—its immensity and its fathomless mystery gripped him with a feeling of grandeur.

Yet he had never been far outside the Solar system. The latter was not necessary on his training cruises, since all the details of a pilot's job—the branch of the Service he had hoped to enter—were the same for both interplanetary and inter-stellar travel. It was the navigator's job that was the harder and more complicated on the longer, faster trips to destinations one could not see when blasting off.

This *"Hellene"* on which he was to ride was about sixty-five feet in diameter and approximately three times that in length. The propulsion was, the builders and engineers acknowledged, not the ultimate by any means. They were still constantly experimenting and hoping for much swifter travel. Still, they did pretty well.

They had some measure of anti-gravity to help lift the ship from a planet. About 22%, Hanlon remembered. They still had to use rockets when near a planet—but these present-day rockets were a far cry from the early crude ones with which Snyder and his men had put first ships on the Moon and planets. These could deliver a thrust far more powerful than those early ones.

For long distances they used a type of "warping" that made the ship "skip" along the lines of force that permeate all space. Hanlon had never quite got it firmly fixed in his mind just how this was done, especially the technique of

40

the engines that made it possible. That was "advanced stuff" that the cadets were not taught in their regular courses—it was Post Graduate work for those who were to become Engineering Masters.

As he went up the escalator into the ship Hanlon was met at the outer lock by a deck steward who led him toward the level where his cabin was located.

This was Hanlon's first time aboard one of these luxury liners—how different the deep-piled rugs, the magnificently frescoed passageway walls, the deeply upholstered furniture, from the utiltarian plainness of the Corps' warships on which he had made his practice cruises.

"As you may know, sir," the steward said as they walked along, "there is neither night nor day in space, but we use Terran time on the ship, and lights are turned on and off to conform to the regular Terran day. Breakfast is served from seven to nine, luncheon from twelve to fourteen, and dinner from eighteen to twenty-one."

"Thanks." A credit note changed from hand to hand—tipping was still in style. The obsequious steward gave him further directions for finding the games and recreational rooms, and other points of interest aboard.

Hanlon unpacked, and stored his luggage in the compact closets and then, having heard the first and second warnings, hastened to the observation desk, to watch the take-off. He had barely reached it and been strapped into the acceleration chair turned to face the long, narrow quartzite port, when the blast-off sirens began screaming their third and final warning.

The intra-ship communicators blared, "All passengers and personnel strap in. Five minutes until blast-off . . . four minutes . . . three . . . two . . . one . . . thirty seconds . . . fifteen . . . ten . . . five, four, three, two, one, BLAST!"

Dimly heard through the insulated hull was what Hanlon knew to be a tremendous crescendo roar of sound, and he was pushed deep into the resilient spring-cushions of his chair. A constricting band seemed to be clamped on his chest, while at the same time there was a curious feeling that he should weigh less but didn't. That was the peculiar sensation the combination of anti-gravity and the thrust of the rockets always gave.

From experience he knew how to regulate his breathing and to let his muscles and nerves relax as much as possible, so that for him there was but a brief moment of discomfort. Then he was able to watch the scene unfolding before and below him.

The ground and that outward splash of almost-intolerable flame quickly dropped away and within minutes the scene expanded until he was able to see hundreds of square miles of city, country and ocean. Soon he could see the distant mountains; but gradually the scene assumed a dimness of detail that persisted until they were far outside the atmosphere. Then the great continental masses became visible as a whole, but without any smaller details apparent.

Two and a half hours later they were past the Moon, and began building up the tremendous speed that was to take them across inter-stellar depths in a matter of short days. And as Luna shrank to a small sphere behind them, Hanlon felt the acceleration grow constant, so unstrapped himself and got up. He stretched hugely, to relieve the cramped feeling in his muscles, then turned to survey his fellow passengers.

He noticed several men in Corps' uniform, and hoped none of them knew him—or if so, would be good enough not to spread word of his disgrace. That would make the trip uncomfortable, lonely and unproductive, for then it would be better for him to spend most of his time in his stateroom. He thought of those "interesting people" he had been told about . . . whatever that tip might mean.

For George Hanlon, youngest man ever to be assigned to the Inter-Stellar Corps' Secret Service—although he did not know this until later—had that within him which placed matters of duty uppermost in his mind at all times.

Accustomed for nearly half of his life to the conscious task of keeping his mind-reading talent hidden and unused, he now knew he must work at it continuously to bring it up to its highest possible level of efficiency. Only by thus knowing every facet of his ability could he do what had to be done in his new task.

He sat down again and closed his eyes in order better to study this problem without outside and extraneous matters interfering. He became awed and a little frightened as he realized fully the weight of his new duties and responsibilities, even though he had been all through this several times before. Somehow, his being aboard ship on his way to his actual work seemed to make this terrific responsibility more weighty.

Why must he be burdened with such a load as they had tied onto him? What were the Corps' top brass thinking of, anyway, to put so much on an untried kid just out of school?

At last he began to think less of his own burden and to concentrate on seeing what he could pick up mentally. He kept his eyes closed, but opened his mind wide and let the welter of thought-impressions roll in unhindered.

There was much laughter and lighthearted gaiety about him, as was natural on such a luxury liner. There was also some fear of space and the emptiness; some actual illness from space-fright. There were many mental undercurrents, and in one or two instances he thought he caught vague hints of sinister intrigue, but was never quite able to isolate these, or to bring them into more distinct focus. Quite evidently the men—or women—thinking such thoughts were able to close their minds to some extent— or else he was too rusty at reading. He realized, too, that they might not be thinking of any such thing—he remembered once when he was a boy he thought he had caught some such thought, then found later it was merely a neighbor reading a story with a sinister plot.

Mind-reading, he told himself, was the field in which he would be assigned to work. The Corps and the SS would be sure to hand him all the jobs where other agents had failed, just as they had in this case, in hopes that he could get them some beginning points of contact. So it was up to him to get busy and learn how to do it better.

The call for lunch found him still studying, but he was hungry, and went down to eat. He could work there as well as on the observation deck, anyway.

Going into the dining room, the head waiter assigned him to a table almost in the center of the large and tastefully decorated room. For some moments he busied himself studying the menu, and when he had ordered he glanced up again at his tablemates.

He had been introduced to this matron, and to her son who appeared to be about his own age. He probed briefly, finding her a good sort but a little too impressed with her own importance—new-rich, he guessed. The boy he disliked on sight—he seemed a selfish, pampered brat.

So he forgot them and concentrated on letting his mind roam about the great room, seeking information and trying to refine and develop his mind-reading ability. It seemed to him the latter was improving to some extent . . . yet realized this could as easily be wish-fulfillment as actuality.

After luncheon he returned to the observation deck and there, as the long afternoon slowly passed, he sat in his deck chair, eyes closed, mind wide open.

Several times he caught some one thought-impression more distinctly than the general run, and concentrated on trying to trace it mentally; to read it more clearly and minutely. But as he did not have much success, it began to irritate him . . . and that made him angrier.

"Keep at it, and don't expect miracles," he scolded himself. "Sure, you've got something, but anything—any ability of mind or muscle—needs training and practice to get anywhere!"

After dinner that first evening Hanlon went into the recreation hall. There were dozens of tables where people were playing various games. He saw that around many of these other people were standing, watching the play, and knew from this that social custom on the ship did not frown on such silent kibitzing.

Therefore, he wandered about until he found a table where four men were playing stud poker. Here he stood, watching the game, but concentrating on the mind of the man opposite him, checking his mental impressions against the man's wins and losses.

He couldn't, at any time, actually read in the man's mind what his "hole card" was, he found. But he could quite easily sense from the player's mind whether the latter considered it a good one, a very poor one, or only a possible winner. By watching the play as well as studying the man's feelings, facial movements and muscle twitches or tensenesses, Hanlon was soon able to make some remarkably accurate predictions as to what the card was.

By checking his deductions with the card when it was shown, he saw he was gradually coming closer and closer to a perfect score of "reading."

The next day Hanlon again sat most of the time in the lounge, his eyes closed, letting his mind soak up all the impressions and vibrations he could. When one seemed particularly strong, he tried to follow it and locate the person—with his mind, not his eyes—and read the whole thought.

Mostly he found again excitement and pleasure. Almost everyone on board seemed to be having a grand time, and enjoying the trip to the utmost. It was what might be expected—a gay, carefree holiday crowd.

Yet there was, occasionally caught, that sinister undercurrent that had so puzzled him since he first sensed it the day before. It was not prominent at any time, nor continuous . . . more as though only one or two minds held the thought, and those not in the lounge all the time, but wandering in and out.

He tried to analyze the feeling of those thoughts. They were malevolent—that he had sensed from the beginning. And finally, later in the afternoon, the person or persons thinking them evidently spent some time near him in the lounge, for the feeling became much clearer to the SS man.

Hanlon still kept his eyes closed. He made no effort at this time to try to identify who was giving out those menacing sensations. That would come later. At the moment he was more interested in trying to work out just what those sinister impressions meant.

And gradually his mind was forced to the conclusion that it could mean only one thing—a killing.

Hanlon was devoting almost all his mind to this problem when another mental impression intruded, and grew stronger, more demanding of his attention.

It was a feeling of symphathetic concern, yet diffident, apologetic. He felt it growing stronger, seeming to be approaching him, to be directed at him.

For the moment he left off worrying about the other matter, and watched this new thought.

By the instant it was growing stronger, and closer. He

knew that, some way. He directed his attention toward what he believed was its source, but idly, half angry at it for interrupting his more important thoughts. It was in front of him . . . and suddenly, like a bright, white beam of light, his mind reached out and touched directly the mind holding that thought.

Touched it . . . it was instantly, unbelievably, *inside* that mind!

He was able, actually, to *read* the surface thoughts!

Clearly, distinctly, as though it were his own mind, Hanlon knew he was one with a deck steward, who had noticed him sitting there all day and the day before, with closed eyes and strained face. (His efforts at concentration must have been too apparent—he'd have to learn to guard that; to keep his face more impassive.)

Now the steward was coming to see if he was ill. And at that instant a soft, apologetic voice spoke from in front of him—spoke words he had already read in that mind.

"Beg pardon, Mr. Hanlon, sir, but is anything wrong?"

He opened his eyes lazily, and let a smile break out as he saw the solicitous face of the white-coated attendant.

"Me? Not really. Just a little queazy, but I'm feeling better all the time."

"I'm glad. But be sure and call if I can be of any service."

"Thank you, I will." Hanlon reached in his pocket and slipped a credit note into the man's hand.

And as the steward walked away Hanlon's mind was instantly whirling with this newly-discovered ability. He was astonished and delighted, of course . . . but a little disturbed, too.

"I was actually inside the guy's mind!" he thought in amazement. "That's a new one! I was never able to do that before. I really read his thoughts! I've got to find out more about this. Let's see, now, how did I do it?"

# Chapter 7

**G**EORGE HANLON GLANCED ABOUT THE OBSER-vation deck and saw at same distance the young man who had sat at the same dining table. Hanlon grinned a bit, and directed his mind that way.

To the best of his memory, he concentrated on doing the same thing he had done when he got inside the steward's mind. For long, anxious minutes he tried. He felt tense, and the strain made his heart pound. At last he sank back into his chair.

"The other was just a fluke, I guess," he frowned in frustration and disgust at himself. "I keep thinking I'm getting good—then flooie!" He idly sent his mind towards the boy again . . . and suddenly found himself once more within another person's mind.

It was a strange, weird feeling . . . this getting two sets of thoughts at the same time. Also, Hanlon felt a bit as though he was a trespasser in some forbidden temple. Yet he persevered, trying to see if he could read anything there . . . and was disappointed to find he could peruse and understand only the fleeting surface thoughts.

With all his might, in every way he could think of, he tried to probe back and beneath those passing thought-concepts, but could get no information whatever of the young man's past or knowledge. Only vacuous, self-centered thoughts which were flowing idly through the youth's mind were available to him.

He wondered if he could influence the other to do something. If he could control another's mind—even just a little—it would really help in his work. So he now tried every method his agile mind could imagine, to make the fellow pick up the book that lay beside his chair. He

47

concentrated on it, he insisted, he willed it. But in vain —he could make no impression whatever.

Hanlon withdrew his mind. "I've no control," he thought to himself. "I can't take over his mind in any way. Neither can I read his past; just his present thoughts. That's not too bad, although I hoped I had hit the jackpot at last."

After some further reflection the thought occurred, "Maybe I can do better with someone else."

During the balance of the day he kept trying to read the minds of others of his fellow passengers, but found the same results in each case. He did, however, develop the technique of making a much quicker entrance into a mind—could do that reading more swiftly, and yet know he was correct.

"I get it now. I've got to approach it relaxed, not all tensed up like I was at first," he finally realized.

But when it came to probing into and reading the whole mind, into its past thoughts and knewledges, no. Just that . . . no!

Pessimistically he began to feel he wasn't going to be able to do as much with his "mind-reading" as he—and his superiors—had hoped.

Did this mean, he wondered disconsolately as he went to his stateroom, that he was to be a failure in the Secret Service? Or, he brightened momently, could he develop other methods of ferreting out information? But that, he told himself honestly, was out. What did he know about detective work? The SS already had the best detectives in the Universe.

This dark mood persisted while he went to bed and finally dropped off to sleep. But when he awoke the next morning he felt cheerful again. He had a lot—and he would get more.

He ate a good breakfast, then went back to his deck chair and there, resolutely, he opened his mind once more to general impressions. He would keep working at it, and more was bound to come. Look how far he'd advanced already. A lot further than when he had started. And at that, he probably—no, undoubtedly—could do more than any of the other fellows on certain problems. As far as he knew—and Dad and Admiral Rogers had talked as though he were the only one they knew about—no one else could read even surface thoughts.

So he kept diligently at it. And very soon, so strongly he deduced the mind must be very close to him, he again found those sinister impressions that had bothered him so much.

This time he glanced about, in apparently casual curiosity, yet touched mind after mind of those nearest him. Then hit pay dirt!

Why, it was that bluff, hearty-looking, red-headed man in the third chair to his right. He didn't look vicious, that was certain, though there was a grim set to his jaw. Yet his surface thoughts showed the man to be hard, cold and ruthless—a pure killer type. Hanson sensed he was one of those men who have such a will to power that the lives and rights of others are held cheaply, contemptuously. The kind who, if another gets in his way, removes him . . . but carefully, lest his own highly-valuable skin bc put in jeopardy. If he could get some one else to do the dirty work, so much the better. Such conscienceless killers were, Hanlon knew, usually arrant cowards.

There was someone on this ship who was in this man's way—of that Hanlon felt sure. The killer was determined to destroy this other the first chance he got. His mind was now weighing chances and possible opportunities—and Hanlon read and learned.

Yes, this must be one of those "interesting people" that unknown SS tipster back on Terra had mentioned. Was the victim another? Probably. For Hanlon had not yet read any thoughts in this killer's mind about any confederates.

Hanlon kept close watch on this man and his mind, and picked up many other stray bits of information, including his name, Panek. None seemed of too much immediate importance regarding the matter at hand. Yet they gave the Secret Service man a fairly good picture of the assassin's personality, when pieced all together.

Suddenly, and but a barely passing whisper of thought, Hanlon caught the concept that the intended victim's death was necessary to the coup "they" were planning on Simonides.

Hanlon was instantly alerted by that planet-name. Perhaps this was a definite lead for him. He strained to get more. The killer thought occasionally of a man he called "The Boss", but not the name of that dignitary, nor his actual position—politically, socially, economically, or otherwise.

The SS man fumed inwardly because he could not get a clear picture of that "Boss." This murderer did not have a visual type of mind, darn it. He didn't see clearly in pictorial terms any of the people or scenes about which he thought.

Hanlon had been gradually impressed, though, with the realization that this man was very much afraid of his boss. There was a mental shiver every time thought of his employer entered his mind. There was something about a previous failure, and what would undoubtedly happen unless it was done now, but Hanlon couldn't get enough of that to make any sense to him.

Again Panek began thinking, though very sketchily, about "Sime", as he called Simonides, and the "plot" that was being hatched there. Hanlon felt the man's sneering contempt for "those beasts"—but could gain no idea whatever about what that reference meant.

In so many ways this puzzle seemed to be growing worse instead of better, and Hanlon knew a moment of frustration. But his sense of humor came to his rescue. "You want the whole thing written out for you in black and white?" he jeered at himself. "Snap out of it! Quit being a defeatist."

Harder and more intently he tried to probe into the man's mind. Oh, if he could only learn to read below those passing surface thoughts; to follow them down and back along the memory-chains into the total mind! Revealing though the thoughts he could catch were, for complete and swift results he must find the technique of reading a mind completely. If such a thing were possible.

But probe as he might, the way to those deeper, buried memories and thoughts continued to remain locked from him.

And then Panek got up and left the observation deck.

A light touch on his knee some time later snapped George Hanlon's eyes wide open, and he looked down to see a small, wriggly dog looking up into his face, its tail frantically wig-wagging signals of proffered friendship, the little tongue making licking motions toward the hand the puppy could not quite reach.

"Well, hi, fellow," Hanlon reached down and lifted the little dog onto his lap, where the latter wriggled and contorted in an ecstasy of joy, climbing all over the young man, licking at his hands and trying to reach his face. The puppy was so extremely happy and anxious to make friends that Hanlon was soon laughing almost convulsively while trying to avoid those well-meant but very moist kisses.

"Wait now, boy. Take it easy. I like you and all that, but let's not get carried away with ourselves."

Hanlon scratched the puppy behind one of its floppy ears, and pressed it firmly but gently down so it was lying on his lap.

"That's better. Just lie there and take it easy."

A sudden thought brought a grin onto the young man's lips. He tried to get into the puppy's mind . . . and got a real surprise. For after a few anxious moments of testing and trying, he did it—actually got the dog's thoughts of pleasure at finding such a wonderful new friend with such a nose-appealing effluvium. Hanlon then tried to see if he could get into the deeper parts of the dog's mind, and using what knowledge of the technique he had deduced in his previous though unsuccessful attempts with humans, found after many more anxious minutes he could follow the thought-and-memory tracks back and back until the dog's whole mind was open to him.

The puppy had far more of a mentality than Hanlon had ever guessed dogs had—and he knew they were far from stupid. This one's mind, he could now see, was immature but latently capable.

Say, this was great! Hanlon probed some more, and found many sketchy facts—sketchy because the thoughts were incomplete to the puppy, beyond its experience, and not because the man couldn't read perfectly what was there. The dog apparently knew a woman—Hanlon got the impression of skirts—and answered when that goddess called the word "Gypsy."

"Gypsy, eh?" Hanlon said aloud, and immediately the dog wriggled from beneath his restraining hand, and again tried to climb up and lick Hanlon's face in a frenzy of adoration.

"Lie down, sir, and be quiet!" Hanlon said sternly, and the puppy did so instantly, without question or hesitation.

Hanlon thrilled, realizing at once that it was not what he had said that did the trick—but the fact that he was still inside the dog's mind, and that it had obeyed his will rather than his words.

"Hey, this needs looking into!"

Without saying the words aloud this time, Hanlon commanded the dog—or rather, he impressed the command directly onto the puppy's mind with his own—to get down off his lap onto the deck.

Instantly it leaped down.

"Lie down." The dog did so.

"Roll over." Again silently. But now the puppy merely looked up at him, imploringly, quivering in an apparent emotion of indecision. Hanlon realized the puppy didn't know *how* to "roll over."

"Guess I need to learn how to do it before I can teach, or rather, command, him to do it," Hanlon grinned wryly to himself. For he realized that to do so he would have to learn how to control each of the dog's muscles, and that before he could do that he would have to know what part of the brain controlled the nerves that made those muscles obey his commands.

And that, if possible at all, would take one galaxy of a lot of study and practice.

For the next several minutes, then, he concentrated in making the puppy do a number of simple tricks, all the time watching carefully to see, if possible, the connecting links between brain, nerves and muscles.

He was beginning to make a little headway in understanding this triple co-relation, when he heard a sudden gasp. He looked up to see a young matron standing before him, her mouth and eyes wide with surprise.

"Why . . . why, Gypsy never did any tricks before. What are you, an animal trainer?"

Hanlon leaped to his feet. "The best in the Universe, Madam," he grinned. "That's a mighty fine puppy you have. He came over and introduced himself, and we've been having some fun together."

"Yes, he ran off, and I've been hunting all over for him. But how on earth did you ever teach him so quickly."

"It's a gift," Hanlon mocked, then grew serious. "Honestly, Madam, I don't know," he said quietly. "I just seem to have a way with dogs, is all. By the way, would you sell me the puppy?"

"Sell Gypsy? No, thanks," and she started away, calling to the dog to follow. But it stood in indecision, looking from one to the other, not seeming to know whether to follow its beloved mistress or to stay and play with this nice new friend.

Hanlon quickly reached out to the dog's mind and impressed on it that it must follow the woman, and always do whatever she told it. The puppy then trotted away, content.

George Hanlon sank into his deck chair. This required a good think—a mighty serious think—he told himself. He would have to work on this as much as on human minds. For if he could control animals—would it work on birds, or insects? Maybe even fish?—then he could get into places he, as a man, could not go.

The lady and dog had disappeared when Hanlon got the inspiration to see if his mind could find them; if he could again contact the dog when it was not in sight, and he did not know exactly where it was.

Instantly, effortlessly, it seemed, as though it happened merely because he wished it to, he found himself again inside the puppy's mind. Was it because he already knew that mind's pattern, he wondered?

Anyway, there he was, and now he tried to see if he could look out through Gypsy's eyes . . . and after much study, he did so. But the vision was so distorted he wondered if his control was at fault, then remembered having heard, or read somewhere, that a dog's eyes do not work exactly the same as a man's.

Finally he accustomed himself to them enough so he could see that they were going down a narrow corridor, and then they stopped before a door, which opened after a moment. The dog, without a command, leaped through the doorway into the stateroom and ran to its basket, where it lay, panting, looking up at its mistress.

# Chapter 8

**G**EORGE HANLON WITHDREW FROM THE PUPPY'S mind, and thought seriously. Yes, this matter of controlling the minds of animals was one that would require a lot of thought and study, and a tremendous amount of practice. But it seemed important enough to justify those expenditures.

He hunted up his steward. "Where do the passengers keep their pets?"

"Some keep them in their staterooms, sir, but others in the kennels down on 'H' deck."

"Thanks. Any rules against my going down there and looking at 'em? I like animals, especially dogs."

"Oh, no, sir. Anyone can go down there. It's on the right hand side, about halfway aft."

Arrived at the kennels, Hanlon found the cages contained about a dozen dogs of various breeds, ages and sizes. Here were plenty of animal minds for his experimentation and study.

After walking around and looking at them for some minutes, he sat down on a bench at one side of the cages, and concentrated on the dog nearest him. It was a large white bull, and he guessed its age to be about five or six years. That was just what he wanted—an adult mind to study, not that of an immature puppy.

He had no trouble getting into the dog's mind, and for over an hour he sat there, studying it line by line, channel by channel, connector by connector, while the dog lay as if asleep. Gradually Hanlon began to feel he was beginning to know something about a dog's mind-and-body correlation, and how it operated.

Then, and only then, he woke the dog and began experiment with control. He found it easy to make the dog do anything he wished that was within the animal's previous knowledge and experience. What he wanted was to see if he could make it perform motions and actions that were outside its previous conditioning and training. After some fumbling, he thrilled to find that now even some of the simpler of those things were not too difficult, although others his present knowledge was not up to handling.

His study taught him to some extent how to activate the brain centers which controlled the nerves that sent messages to the proper muscles that allowed the dog to do his bidding. But it still needed a lot of study. He knew he had only made a bare start at learning what had to be known to do it swiftly and easily.

The kennel steward must have noticed the strange antics of the bull and then, seeing Hanlon's intent concentration, figured there might be some conection between the two. For he came up to the bench and looked down somewhat hostilely at the man sitting there. But his voice, when he spoke, was very polite.

"Anything I can do for you, sir?"

Hanlon had been concentrating so deeply he had not heard anyone come up, and the voice, speaking so suddenly right before him, startled and befuddled him. He looked up, and his mind felt sluggish and weak, almost as though he had been doped.

"Huh?" he asked stupidly.

"I asked," the man's tone was a little sharper, "if there was anything I could do for you?"

"Oh, no. No thanks." Hanlon forced himself to pay attention. "I just like dogs and came down here to watch them. Must have dozed off."

"Do you have a dog of your own here?"

"No, I have no dog at present."

"What were you doing to that white bull. He's been acting very peculiar since you've been here."

"Me?" Hanlon made himself look surprised. "Why, nothing. I've just been sitting here; haven't said a word to any of them."

"Well, I'm not too sure it's proper for you to be here as long as you have no dog kennelled here."

"Sorry. If it bothers you, I'll leave."

Hanlon started away . . . then stopped short. He had

wondered at that curiously sluggish feeling in his mind. Now, with a start he had trouble concealing, he suddenly realized a mind-numbing fact!

He had seen and heard that exchange of conversation from two separate and distinct points! And now he was watching himself leave!

*He had heard and seen both from his own . . . and from the dog's mind!*

Yes, he suddenly comprehended that the dog had heard and understood every word of that brief conversation—not as a dog might, *but as a man would!*

Suddenly drenched with a cold sweat, Hanlon knew he had not merely been inside the dog's mind, observing and controlling, but that he had actually *transferred* a portion of his own mind into the dog's brain!

No wonder his own mind—what was left in his own brain—had felt somewhat inadequate and lacking for the moment. It was not his complete mind. When the steward startled him, he had forgotten to withdraw from the bull's brain.

Now he carefully did so, and with senses reeling, almost ran back to his stateroom.

Hanlon threw himself onto the bed and lay there, trembling with awe at realization of the immensity of what he had done.

How in the name of Snyder was such a thing possible? Reading a mind's impressions, even the surface thoughts, was well within the realms of possibility he knew, for he had done it himself. Even hundreds of years before, such things had been believed possible, and had been studied extensively and scientifically. Many people throughout the centuries had claimed the ability to read minds, though only a few had ever proven their powers satisfactorily under carefully controlled laboratory conditions.

He himself, until the past day or so, had not been able to read a mind directly, nor could he do it perfectly even yet, with humans.

Also, he conceded, it was a reasonable concept that if he had any mental ability at all with humans, it should be greater and more efficient with animals. For they had less actual brain-power; their minds were far less complex than human minds.

But to be able to transfer part of his mind . . . to separate it—dissociate it—and have it outside of his body and in some other body's mind!

"Ain't that sumpin'?" he whistled in awed amazement.

Pulling himself together with an effort of will, he set his mind to reviewing carefully the entire episode, and to figuring out where all this might fit in with the business at hand.

"I thought, when I first got into that pup's mind, that it would be a big help, and it will. But this will be even more so, if I can really control animals, and see and hear with their eyes and ears. And if I can send them where I want them to go, and send my mind, or part of it, along with them, and still know what it and they are doing, that will be tremendous!"

He remembered how he had been able to get into the puppy's mind after it had gone out of sight, so now he sent his mind down to the kennels. Again, without any trouble, without any delay or hesitation, he found himself inside the bull's mind, and could look out through the cage wires and see the rest of the kennel deck.

He withdrew and lay there, almost dumbfounded.

"How did I ever get such ability?" he wondered. "No one else in our family has it. Am I some sort of a mutant? But if so, how or why? I never heard Dad or Mother mention it."

He had lots of questions, but no answers.

But thinking about this new ability and his job with the Secret Service suddenly reminded him of that potential murderer he had been watching. He realized with dismay that in his excitement over this latest development he had entirely forgotten that angle. He had better get back on the ball, but fast!

He got up, splashed cold water on his face, dried it, ran a comb through his hair, and went back to the lounge.

The man Panek was not in the Observation lounge, so Hanlon went seeking him. Just as he neared the game rooms on his rounds, he saw his man leaving them. Allowing the stranger to get some distance ahead, Hanlon trailed him as carefully as he could, all the time trying to read what the killer had in mind.

Not entirely to his surprise, Hanlon found he could now read the surface thoughts even more easily than formerly. Thus he soon knew, emphatically, that the man was definitely bent on that contemplated killing right now—that the victim was in his stateroom but was going to leave it shortly in response to a faked video-call.

Hanlon also learned that the murderer had a knife concealed in his sleeve—and was adept in its use.

The SS man's mind rocketed swiftly. What was he to do? He didn't want a murder done, but neither did he want this man killed nor jailed—at least not until he had learned a great deal more concerning him and his part in or knowledge of that "plot" on Simonides that Hanlon and the Corps were trying so desperately to solve.

"I've got to learn to consider mighty carefully all the angles about even the most apparently-insignificant things," he thought carefully. "I can't take chances of gumming things up, but on the other hand, I want to get an 'in' with that gang if I can."

A possibility occurred to the young agent—and he quailed a bit, then grinned wolfishly at the thought. It was plenty dangerous, but if he could put it over maybe it would give him that "in" he needed.

He hurried his steps and caught up with the big man just as the latter was stopping momentarily to peer cautiously around the corner and down a corridor which, Hanlon could read in his mind, led to the victim's stateroom.

Hanlon tapped the man on the shoulder, and as the fellow whirled, a snarl on his face, Hanlon stepped backward a pace and held up his hands in the "I'm not armed" gesture. Then, before Panek could speak, he stepped closer to whisper.

But the thug was both angry and frustrated at the spoiling of his carefully-worked-out plan, and in no mood for conversation. That lethal knife seemed to jump out of his sleeve and toward Hanlon, in the strong, swift, practiced hand of the killer.

The SS man jumped backward, then his own hands darted out and grabbed for the other's wrists in the manner he had been taught. He caught the right, or knife hand, but the big fellow was as dextrous as he, even if he didn't look capable of such fast action. His other hand eluded Hanlon's grasp, and with it Panek struck and jabbed —heavy blows to Hanlon's face and body.

Hanlon parried the blows as best he could, at the same time trying to make his low-voiced words penetrate.

"Cut it out, you fool! I'm trying to help you, not hinder you! Stop it, blast you, and listen!"

But he might as well have been talking to the metal walls. One eye was swelling rapidly, and he had a nick in his arm that he could feel was soaking his jacket sleeve. Seeing he couldn't make the fellow listen, Hanlon threw him with a super-judo trick, then sat on him.

"Shut up and listen to me, Panek!" he hissed urgently, using all his fighting technique meanwhile to keep the other's threshing form immobile. "I'm trying to warn you that the bozo you're after carries one of those new needle-guns, and the needles are poison-tipped. Also, he's the fastest man on the draw I've ever seen—I watched him practice. Just one of those needles and you'd be kaput before you could yell."

"Why . . . how . . . what d'you mean, huh, what d'you mean?"

The man stopped his struggles for the moment, while his face showed plainly how aghast he was at this interfering stranger's apparent knowledge of his intentions.

"Who are you, huh, and what's your game, what's your game?"

Hanlon made his voice seem both friendly and calculating, and hurried on with his specious explanation before the fellow should start fighting again.

"I'd been tipped off there was something up, on Simonides, where a good hustler could make himself plenty of credits. And credits in quantity is what I'm after . . ."

"What's that got to do with me, huh, what has it?"

". . . and I'm on my way there to see what my chances are of getting in on the game. So naturally I tried to learn all I could about it ahead of time. I was told this bird you're after was an important man there, so I studied him. One of the first things I found out about him was that he carried one of those needlers. If he's in your way, together we oughta be able to get rid of him . . . but let's play it safe, eh?"

The stranger gave him a cold, calculating going-over with those hard, suspicious eyes. "Let me up, Bub, let me up. I'll be good while we talk."

Hanlon rose, but stood warily as the other slowly climbed to his feet. But he wasn't sharp enough—Panek's hand flashed out even before he seemed to be standing erect, and slickly grabbed the wallet from the inside pocket of Hanlon's jacket.

But the SS man, seeing what the other was after, stood there without making any resistance.

"Take your time looking at 'em, Pal," he said easily. "I'm clean. Strictly on my own in this. Just got kicked out of that snake's nest of a Corps school on Terra . . ."

The killer's head snapped up at mention of the Corps, and he stared harder and more suspiciously than ever into Hanlon's eyes.

". . . They said I cheated at exams, and wouldn't give me a chance to defend myself," Hanlon continued quickly, but with heat. "That soured me on 'em, but good! So I says to myself, blast John Law! From now on I'm on the other side. Anything he's after must be worth plenty to any guy who can outsmart him. Knowing his side of it and how he works, I figure I'm just that good!"

He said all this with such a deadly serious voice, that although it was bravado Panek could see it was also confidence. Hanlon had figured this straight-forwardness was his best bet. Tell his side of it first, for if he got in with them—or any gang—they would be sure to check, and would find out he had been a cadet, anyway. "Beat 'em to the punch before they form any contrariwise conclusions," was his judgment.

His plan seemed to be working, for as his explanation continued and was completed the killer looked at him with some measure of respect, although his eyes and manner were still filled with suspicion.

"Can't blame you for feeling sore, can't blame you, if they really did kick you out. But I don't trust nobody that's ever had any connection at all with the cops, don't trust 'em!"

"Look, Pal, use your head! If I was a John Law would

I merely have stopped you? I'd be arresting you—or killing you for pulling that knife on me. I tell you I'm clean—and that I want an 'in' on Simonides."

"I heard, too, there was good pickings on Sime," the man said slowly. " 'Course, I'm not in on anything special, myself, not in on it. This here's a purely personal grudge deal. But you prob'ly did me a good turn, a good turn, and if you want to look me up after we land, I maybe could introduce you to a man or two. I didn't know old Abrams carried one of them needlers, didn't know that."

The thanks in his gruff voice showed his respect for those silent, deadly little guns.

That name—Abrams—rang a bell in Hanlon's mind, though he quickly decided he'd better let it lie for the moment—file it away for future investigation.

He smiled in comradely fashion. "The way you were walking into it made me sure you didn't know. And thanks. Maybe I will look you up. I don't know anyone on Simonides, and it doesn't hurt to have a friend or three. Where do I find you there?"

"Evenings I'm often at the Bacchus Tavern. And," with a sinister grimace, "if you come, you'd better pray that 'he' likes you, you'd sure better!"

# Chapter 9

S MAN GEORGE HANLON WENT SLOWLY BACK to his room where he could think seriously without the outside abstractions he would be sure to encounter in any of the public rooms.

He had made a good bid, he thought, for contact with what he felt sure must be the group he wanted to get in with. Hanlon felt Panek's statement that he, personally, was not in on it, was just so much hog-wash. That last crack about "you'd better pray that 'he' likes you," was almost sure proof.

But what did it mean? Who was this "he," and why had Hanlon better pray "he" liked him? Probably the leader . . . and if so, undoubtedly a dangerous man to play around with. Hanlon remembered the fear of his boss he'd read in Panek's mind.

Also, what about Abrams? Hanlon felt sure it was the same man he had guarded that day. Oh, oh, was that "failure" he had also read in Panek's mind that unsuccessful attempt he, Hanlon, had thwarted? Was Panek— and through him this as-yet-unmet leader—behind that attempt on Abrams' life?

These were questions he could not answer yet—not enough data. But he would have to find the answers sometime. And once in Panek's gang, he might find them. And even if this particular gang was not the one doing the plotting in which the Corps was so interested, Hanlon felt that getting into even one of the organized gangs on Simonides would be a step in the right direction.

But he would have to watch his step. Those fellows would be about as safe to play with as a pitful of cobras. For a long moment he grew cold with fear; a deadly, paralyzing terror that twisted his vitals into hard, hard knots. What business did he have, mixing with mature, deadly killers such as these?

On the other hand, he consoled himself after awhile, being able to read their surface thoughts should warn him when he started getting out of line. Then, if or when he did, he would walk more softly, travel inch by inch, and not make any attempts to jump into the big middle of things until he got a lot more information . . . and more experience in the ways and means of gangsterism.

But suddenly he felt that cold fear return. Those men were—must be—hard, trained killers all. This Panek was not even the boss—was just a gunny. And those higher-ups would be much worse than Panek—more ruthless and more contemptuous of human life and rights. They would have to be, to be the higher-ups. For Hanlon sensed that in such a group, Might very decidedly made Right . . . and Power.

It took some time to quiet his shrieking nerves. Nor

did he ever forget the awfulness of that fear that so nearly brought him down out of control. On the other hand, never again did he reach such depths of utter panic.

He finally rose, bathed and dressed for dinner. But during the meal his mind was in such a turmoil he had trouble keeping himself outwardly calm. For the first time in more years than he could remember he merely toyed with his food . . . and he had always been a good trencherman.

But he had something very important to do tonight, and he would let nothing keep him from it. So he went to the *Hellene's* library and studied from such books on biology and physiology as he could find, all he could about the brain and the nerves that formed the connecting links between it and the muscles. He studied until the dimming of the lights told him that "day" was over.

He then sent his mind down into the brain of the bulldog, and watched through its eyes until he saw the kennel steward leave for the night. Then Hanlon went down to the kennel deck.

Sitting on the same bench as before, Hanlon sent his mind into that of the white bull. Again he had no trouble attaching a portion of his mind to the dog's brain. A little experimentation soon showed how much of his mind that brain could contain.

Then, from the *inside*, he studied that brain line by line, muscle and nerve channels and connectors, even more surely than he had been able to do before.

The first thing he learned, and put into practice, was to make the dog sleep, so he wouldn't tire too much. After nearly three hours of intensive study he was convinced he was beginning to know it quite well, although he realized how much there still was for him to learn—how much study and practice he would need.

He then woke the dog, and while still leaving that part of his mind in its brain, scanned the next cage which held a beautiful female Airedale. Into her brain he sent another portion of his mind. Then into the next dog another portion, and on and on until he had detached more than three-quarters of his mind, and was controlling directly eight dogs.

His body felt weak and listless as it sagged on the

bench, and he made it lie down there in the semi-darkness. There was, he was afraid at the time, little more than enough mind left in his body to keep the semi-automatic functions going.

It was the most weird sensation imaginable, having portions of his mind in nine places at once—having nine different and distinct viewpoints!

He found he could do, although not too well at first, nine different things at once and the same time, or could make all the bodies he was controlling do the same thing at the same time.

He "drilled" the dogs, making them line up, walk left or right or back up, all in unison. He found that while his mind was divided and controlling different bodies, there was a thread of connecting thought between them all, so that he knew what each of the others was doing. Yet it was not a *central* command—each individual mind-portion could and did do its own deciding and commanding.

For hours Hanlon practiced with the dogs until he had worked out the procedure to the point where he knew he could make them perform—singly, as a group, or each doing a different thing—almost any task of which their body muscles were capable, whether they had previously known how to do it or not.

Bringing his mind-portions back from seven of the dogs into his own brain, after commanding them to sleep, he went over to the cage of the Airedale he was still controlling. Squatting down before the bars, he took a pencil-stub and piece of paper from his pocket. These he passed through the bars and laid at her feet.

Then, while he watched with his own mind through his own eyes, he used only the portion of his mind that was inside her brain, and made the Airedale pick up the pencil in her teeth, blunt end inside her mouth. Holding it thus, she attempted to write on the paper, which she held steady with her two front paws.

Anxious minutes passed while Hanlon sweatingly experimented. At last the dog managed to print, very roughly and clumsily, a few letters. They were large and very crude. It wasn't that he couldn't control her muscles—it was simply that the muscles were not built to do such things without infinite training.

When it finally became so near "morning" that he knew he had to quit, Hanlon left the kennels and went to bed. He was still amazed, excited and thrilled about this strange and weird ability, but he was also well content with his studies. If a time came when he might wish or need to use animals in his work, he felt capable of managing them. Yet again he realized how much there was to learn; that he must continue practicing and studying at every opportunity.

Did cats or horses—or birds or insects—have brains that worked the same as the dogs? He would have to experiment to find that out, first chance he got.

But now there was another very serious problem demanding his attention. He had made a wonderful start at getting an "in" with Panek, the Simonidean thug. Now, how could he best turn that to his advantage?

It was some time before he fell asleep from sheer weariness, nor had he solved the problem before he did so.

The moment he awoke, late the next morning, he knew he had the answer. His sub-conscious must have solved it for him while he slept.

At brunch he kept his eyes open, and before too long Panek came into the dining room for his lunch. Hanlon signalled, and his new-found acquaintance came to his table. Their orders given and the waiter on his way, Hanlon opened up.

"Look, Pard, I don't want to butt into your business, but if you want this Abrams out of your way, I'll be glad to take a crack at it for you."

The Simonidean looked at him scornfully. "Think you're that good, eh? Better'n me at bumping off a man, huh? Better'n me?"

"Oh, no," Hanlon made his face seem very apologetic, and his tone the same. "I'm not setting myself even one notch ahead of you, nor criticizing your way of working . . ."

"Better not, neither!"

". . . but every man has his own techniques. Look, in this case, aboard a ship in space where you can't run or hide, I think my way would work best."

The other was becoming interested in spite of himself, and his truculence melted a bit, although his tone was still sneering. "All right, Master Mind, how'd you handle it, how would you?"

"A gun or knife is all right on some jobs," Hanlon leaned closer and spoke in a semi-whisper, but earnestly. "But there are times when it's plain foolish to sneak up behind a man and hit him on the head with a club."

"Yeah, you got something there, got something."

"In such a case, I figure it's a lot better to make friends with the guy, take him to dinner, then sneak a little cyanide in his coffee—something like that."

Panek was impressed. Hanlon read the swift thoughts racing across the other's mind. He hadn't liked the idea of using his knife, here on this ship. But neither did he dare report back to that feared "boss" that he hadn't succeeded in killing Abrams.

Panek spoke doubtfully. "Yeah, that may be all right, but not when the guy knows you, then you can't get away with a thing like that, not when he knows you."

"Exactly what I'm getting at," Hanlon said eargerly. "Me, I'm the Unknown Quantity. Nobody knows me. I can get to old Abrams and make it all seem natural."

"He ain't easy to fool, no, he ain't."

"I'm sure he isn't. But since I've got to make a start somewhere if I want to get into things on Simonides, I figure giving you an assist is worth the trial."

"Well," Panek hesitated and his cold eyes bored into those of this enigmatic young man. "I still don't quite trust you, can't be sure I trust you. I still figure you're some kind of a cop . . ."

Hanlon half-rose, his face dark with intense anger. "Don't ever call me a cop!" he blazed, though still in a whisper. "I hate 'em. As a kid I thought they were tops, and did everything I could to get into their school. But I mighty quick found out how wrong I was. I was good and sick of 'em, and about ready to quit when they threw me out on that lie about cheating . . . say, I knew more'n their knuckle-headed instructors, so why'd I need to cheat?"

"Easy, Pal, take it easy."

"They just want to use their high and mighty authority," Hanlon ignored Panek's shushing. "They just like to push people around 'cause they got on a pretty uniform."

His voice had risen in pitch until Panek had to grab his arm and shake him to make him keep still. People at the nearer table were beginning to look at them. But Panek was impressed now with Hanlon's sincerity—the SS man could read that in his mind.

"All right, Pal, all right. Don't bust a gut. You bump off old Abrams without getting caught, and I'll get you in with a gang on Sime where you can really do yourself some good, really some good."

Hanlon nodded shortly and rose. "I'll keep in touch. And your man's as good as dead right now."

His heart was singing—his plan was working smoothly. Now if that government man had any brains, and would play along . . .

Hanlon found Abrams in the library, and slipped into the seat next to him. Opening a magazine and holding it fairly high before his face while apparently reading it, Hanlon started talking in low but penetrant tones.

"Don't look up, Mr. Abrams, but listen to me. You may or may not know it, but there's a plot against your life. I managed to delay it yesterday, but they intended getting you before we reach port. Now I have a plan. I earnestly beg you to listen and work with me."

The Simonidean had given a slight start when he heard Hanlon's first words, but he had been well-trained in a hard school, and in no other way had even shown that he heard. Now, however, he spoke as guardedly as Hanlon. "Who is trying to kill me?"

"A man named Panek, but someone's behind him that I don't know. But the question is: will you work with me?"

"Yes, if I can."

Abandoning his attempts at secrecy, Hanlon started laughing out loud, as though at something he was reading. As Abrams looked up in surprise, Hanlon leaned over and held out his magazine in front of the Simonidean, pointing at it.

"Play up now," he said softly, and the diplomat, quick on the up-take, pretended to look at what Hanlon was showing him, then began laughing in turn. Thereafter, the ice broken as far as any onlookers might know, the two talked naturally as shipboard acquaintances might do.

"Why," Abrams really looked at Hanlon for the first

time, "you're the young man who saved my life on Terra, aren't you?"

"Yes, but keep it quiet. I want us to stick together more or less the rest of the day, as though we'd just met and liked each other. Then have dinner together. Do you have your own servant?"

"My valet, yes, and he is absolutely trustworthy. Why?"

"While we're eating I'll appear to put something into your drink while you're not looking. A few moments later you'll act as though you were suddenly taken ill, and go to your room. Have your valet later let the word out that you're very ill, and send word by space-video for an ambulance to meet the ship. Just before landing, let him say you've died. The ambulance can take you wherever it's natural your body would be taken, and you keep under cover for some time, until I notify you. Can do?"

"Hmmm." The other thought rapidly but cogently for some minutes. "With a few minor variations, yes. But why? . . . oh, I see. You want to get in with the gang, is that it?" When Hanlon nodded Abrams continued, "you're playing a dangerous game, but that's what we've learned to expect of your Corpsmen. A wonderful group!"

"Thanks." Hanlon did not want to explain anything, so let it go at that, and the two talked companionably of many things as they moved naturally about the ship. They listened for a while to a concert in the music room, then played a few games of cards. Each time the diplomat tried to ask questions, Hanlon side-stepped.

The SS man had seen Panek cautiously spying on them from time to time, and when the two went in to dinner the thug took a seat nearby, but where Abrams could not see him.

Hanlon had been probing Abrams' mind all this time, but had been unable to get any clue as to a plot that might upset the peace of his world, or the Federation. Hanlon realized the man was an intense patriot, and he came to the conclusion that Abrams did not particularly like the Prime Minister. But the "why" of that dislike eluded him.

The two were about finished with dinner and their coffee had been served. Hanlon called his companion's attention to something behind him. As the latter turned to look, Hanlon's hand flashed out and hovered an instant over the other's cup.

A few moments later the Simonidean played his part to perfection. He took a drink, then another, and almost before he had set his cup down, gave a groan, and clutched at his stomach and throat.

He rose shakily, and tottered away heavily on the arm of an anxious steward who had come running up.

Hanlon, although he rose quickly and made his face seem concerned and sympathetic, resumed his seat and finished his coffee. When the steward returned, he called him over, and seemed reassured when the latter reported that Mr. Abrams had said it was apparently only an attack of indigestion, to which he was prone, and that his man could take care of him.

But the next day word ran about the ship that Abrams was very ill, and not expected to live the day out.

Panek sauntered past where Hanlon was sitting, reading, and stopped to ask for a light.

"Nice work, Pal, nice work," he whispered as he was lighting his cigaro. "See me at the Bacchus."

But his thoughts, as Hanlon scanned them, were muttering viciously, "I'll cut out his guts if he's planning to louse up 'his' plans, I'll sure carve him!"

And a bit later, as Hanlon reviewed the entire episode, he thanked his stars that Panek was a lot less than an intellectual giant. A brighter man would have wondered about the source of Hanlon's knowledge of his homicidal plans; and how it happened that Hanlon carried a supply of poison. There had been no indication that either question had occurred to Panek.

# Chapter 10

**T**HE MOMENT HE GOT OFF THE SHIP AND WENT into the city of New Athens he could feel it. There was an air of mystery, of secretiveness, of intrigue, that could not help but be noticed by one as sensitive to emotion-impressions as SS Man George Hanlon.

He got out of his ground-cab at the entrance of a great park in the center of the city, but directed the driver to take his luggage on to the hotel. Then Hanlon went in to sit on a bench beneath a beautiful, flowering ba'amba tree.

Once there, he opened his mind to its fullest extent, and let all the impressions and sensations of this new world soak in. He could not, of course, get any factual details in this way, nor did he expect to. What he wanted, and began to get, was the "feel" of the city. And the longer he sat the less he liked it.

For he could sense so clearly that there most certainly was "a Mercutian in the fuel pit" here somewhere. But what it was; what this strange feeling portended, he could not quite make out.

He noticed, casually, that there were the usual idlers in this park, and hundreds of children with their nurses or parents. But there were none of the derelicts one sees in so many large-city parks. Most of the people seemed well-dressed and not too poor. He could catch occasional bits of thought about big business deals.

After a time Hanlon noticed that here, as in most parks, hundreds of native, pigeon-like birds were flying and hopping about, seeking what crumbs they could scrounge from picnickers' lunches, or nuts fed them by interested idlers.

He wondered if he could get into a bird's mind, and

sent his out to contact one. His ability was, he found, much the same as it had been with the dogs—he could not only "read" what mind the pigeon had, but could control it . . . could actually project part of his mind into the bird's brain.

The brain-texture, was different, but as he sat there for another hour, he learned the difference. For now he knew what to look for, and it did not take long until he knew it well. Finally he got so he could see and understand what the people around him were doing—not through his own direct observation, but through the pigeon's senses. He sent several winging high into the air, and got a good perspective of the entire city.

At last he brought his mind back into his own brain, and gave a mental shrug, then rose from the bench.

"You're just stalling, you know," he scolded himself. "Get to the hotel, check in, then go look in the bank vault. You've got a job to do, so get doing it!"

From the hotel he went to the bank and signed up for a box. There was nothing yet for him in box 1044, so he left a note addressed "To Any SS Man," stating he was here and ready to begin his work.

Back at the hotel he unpacked, took a shower, and then a short nap. There was no telling what the night might bring forth, and he wanted all his strength and powers.

New Athens was a beautiful city, as befitted the capitol of the richest planet in the Federation. For Simonides Four had become just that, even outstripping Terra in the wealth from her manufacturers and exports. Her shipments of ores, jewels, unusual furs, manufactured goods, precision tools and art products, as well as foodstuffs raw and processed, ran into trillions of credits every year.

The great square showed plainly that some architect or city planner with a love of classic lines had been in charge here. The buildings were all modern representations of the great temples and public buildings of the Golden Age of Greece on Terra. They were widely spaced, with magnificent lawns and gardens surrounding each.

Thousands of lights artfully concealed accentuated the beauty of those wonderful buildings, and Hanlon caught his breath in pleasure at his first sight of the marvelous square by night. He had thought it wonderful by day—

now he admitted without reservation that it was the most magnificent sight he had ever seen.

He finally signalled a ground-cab—New Athens had no slideways—to go to the Bacchus. It was several blocks from the square, but each of the streets he travelled were almost as beautiful.

The tavern was housed in a large though one-storied building with a pillared facade. The main room was level with a gardened terrace five steps above the street.

Inside, the tavern was tastefully decorated in subdued colors. It was dimly lighted by representations of flambeaus, stuck at angles in the walls. The center of the room was occupied by dozens of tables of varying sizes, while along one side and part of the back were curtained booths. Along the other side ran an ornate bar.

Hanlon made his way to the latter, and sat on one of the upholstered stools. The bar girls, he noted with interest, were revealingly costumed in pseudo-peplos of a purplish, cob-webby, silkish material. They wore no blouses, but long sashes that passed behind the neck, crossed the breasts and tied about the waist to hold up the short skirt. One of the girls came up to get his order.

"I'm new on the planet," he smiled. "Let me have your best native light wine."

She brought him a glass filled with a sparkling, golden liquid, and waited while he took his first appreciative sip. "We call it 'Golden Nectar'," she smiled.

He smacked his lips. "Wonderful!" Then, as she started away he called her back. "Do you know a Mr. Panek? I was to meet him here, but I don't see him."

Her eyes widened a bit at that name. "I'll see if I can locate him for you, sir," and she moved away.

Some minutes later, while he was still pretending to sip his drink, Hanlon felt a hearty clap on the shoulder.

"Well, well, it's my pal from the ship. Welcome to Sime, Pal, welcome to Sime."

"Hi, Panek! Hope you meant that about looking you up, 'cause here I am."

Hanlon flipped a credit note on the bar and followed Panek. He was led toward a back corner, but there, instead of going into one of the booths, Panek pushed through an almost hidden alcove. He knocked peculiarly on a door, and a peephole was opened. When the guardian saw who it was, the door was opened enough so the two could slide through.

Hanlon, in a quick, comprehensive glance, saw that it was a fairly large office, at present occupied by four men.

"This is George Hanlon," Panek introduced him, "the guy who did that job on old Abrams, the same guy."

Hanlon noticed that Panek did not name the men there, but he could see they appeared to know all about him, and were giving him a close once-over. Hanlon scanned back in return, his mind quickly touching one after another of the three sitting in large, easy chairs. Only their surface thoughts were readable, and he knew at first touch they were but underlings, the same as Panek. He read a favorable impression of himself, but with reservations.

He turned his attention to the well-dressed, impressive-looking man behind the plasticene desk, nor had his other probings taken more than a few seconds. He noted with interest the round, smooth face, the slightly over-large greenish eyes, the silver hair that seemed finer and silkier than any Hanlon had ever seen on a human being. It was almost like fine fur, he thought suddenly.

Then he got a shock! This man was different . . . Hanlon could not touch that mind at all! There was a sort of an . . . an alien feeling there he could not quite fathom. It was like no other mind he had ever tried to read.

But he was careful not to let his face show anything of his inner thoughts as he saluted them gravely after that first brief pause.

Then suddenly he made his face show a boyish enthusiasm . . . almost a naivete. "Maybe Mr. Panek has already told you about me. I'm looking for a chance to make a flock of credits . . . and I'm not too particular how I get 'em."

But his mind was tense and anxious. What was their game? And this fellow behind the desk, this leader. Who was he? Hanlon knew he would have a real job finding out those answers . . . but knew he must!

The leader nodded suavely. "That is a very . . . uh . . . commendable desire," he said in a low, gentle voice that was a perfect match for his outward appearance of high gentility. "We can always use a good man," he continued, "who isn't afraid . . . nor too squeamish."

"A trigger-man?" Hanlon shrugged. "If it pays well, okay."

The man seemed to recoil, his delicate hands fluttering in the air almost femininely. "No, no, my dear young man. You misunderstood me entirely. We do nothing so crude, so vulgar, so . . . so brutal. Oh, sometimes we . . . uh . . . sometimes an accident happens to someone. But nothing, you understand, that we have anything to do with. Your technique with the poor Mr. Abrams, who was so suddenly taken . . . ill . . . had led me to hope you had more finese."

"I beg your pardon," Hanlon's tone was now one of apology. "I can finesse, all right, but I didn't know you wanted me to talk that way in private. I'll remember, and respect your wishes from now on."

Inwardly he was puzzled. He kept trying to touch that mind, but could not. Was the guy human—or did he have a mind-control of some sort? Was he used to mind-reading, so that he had developed a defense against it?

Or—and Hanlon almost caught his breath in momentary fear—was this ape a mind reader? A real one, not a dub like himself?

But the leader was answering, still in that gentle tone, as though nothing had happened. "So . . . so . . . that is good. I hate the thought of bloodshed, and I will not countenance roughness in actions or speech. It is regrettable, of course, that sometimes men are stupid enough to oppose us, but . . ." and again that almost feminine gesture.

This was the silkiest, slimiest . . . thing . . . George Hanlon had ever encountered, and again his heart quailed for the moment. "If I was on my own," he shuddered inwardly, "I'd sure never team up with a guy like that!"

For there was no single iota of mercy or compassion in that ice-cold mind behind that gentle face—of that Hanlon was sure.

There was a long, pregnant moment of silence, while the five men studied Hanlon more carefully. Finally the man behind the desk spoke more slowly. "Perhaps—just perhaps, you understand, and nothing definite as yet—we may have a little job for you before long. On another planet. You have no objections to travel?"

"Not if there's a bundle of the stuff at the end of the trip, no," Hanlon grinned avariciously. But his mind was seeking answers. Why did they want to send him away? Was this a bona-fide job, or a trap? Should he go to some other planet? Would he thus get best leads? Perhaps—if it wasn't for too long a time, of course.

The leader smiled suddenly while Hanlon was thus thinking, and the rest grinned as though they had been waiting for his lead to relax their vigilance. "There will be a very large . . . uh . . . bundle." He paused a moment, then continued "We need more overseers on . . . a certain planet. It is one that is rich in various metals. The natives mine it under our direction, and . . ."

Hanlon interrupted. "I don't know a thing about mining. Will that make a difference?" Here, he thought swiftly, was the test. If they still wanted him—and had a reasonable answer—it might well be a bona-fide job.

"None at all," the leader smiled again. "We have mining engineers in charge. Your job would be merely to keep the natives working at top speed. It is . . . uh . . . unfortunate, that they are high enough in the cultural scale so we cannot, under the Snyder dictum, colonize their planet and work it ourselves. But we will chan . . ." he broke off as though realizing he was saying too much, and Hanlon stiffened inwardly.

This was a real clue. What planet was the man talking about? His most penetrant mind-probing could not get the answer from any of the minds there—to the others it was merely "a planet," nothing more. And this ape, with his perfect mental control, let nothing leak.

But the leader had caught himself and gone on almost as though there had been no break, ". . . chance using you, I think. If so, your salary will be a thousand credits a month, plus all expenses. And a nice bonus every so often, depending on how little trouble you have with your crew, and how much ore they take out."

Hanlon showed that gleam of avarice again. "Sounds

very interesting." Then he leaned forward. "One more thing. How long does the job last?"

"For several years, if you want it, and if we continue to be satisfied with you. But we bring the men back every few months for a vacation. We find that best with most of them—the climate there is not too pleasant, and the conditions are confining."

"Nothing to do but work, eh?"

"Just about that. The shifts are about eight hours of our time, and between them you eat, sleep, read or play cards . . . but you do not explore or anything like that! The ship goes there every three weeks, and we usually figure eighteen weeks there, then the three weeks back here. The guards and others rotate that way. Thy have a tendency to . . . uh . . . deteriorate if we don't."

Hanlon let himself shiver, but grinned as he did so. "Now that's one thing I don't want to do—go nuts. Can't make any credits doing that."

The leader raised his hand. "You understand, of course, there will be a short period of . . . uh . . . checking and testing before we decide to send you out on a job."

Hanlon's voice was almost servile, yet confident. "Sure, sir. You name it; I do it."

He was still probing with everything he had, but still getting nothing important. A couple of the men seemed to be chuckling about what might happen to him if he failed the tests—but he had guessed that much, anyway.

Suddenly the leader leaned across the desk, and his genteel manner slipped from him like a discarded mask. His eyes became glacial ice.

"Don't get any grandiose ideas in your head, Hanlon. We are not fools. Nor are we offering you a chance to get in on our complete plans. I am just, possibly, hiring you to do a simple job."

"Oh, no, sir, I wasn't even thinking of such a thing," Hanlon looked hurt. "Why, I'm just a kid. I know I couldn't expect anything else . . . at first. Not until I've proved myself to you, or until I've made my pile and got in a position of power. Then, naturally, I'd want to get into something where I could really go places. But that's for years and years ahead, I know that."

The now-hard, cold eyes scrutinized him carefully,

but still doubtfully. When the leader spoke his voice was more cordial, though still harder, not soft as it had been at first.

"I'll be frank, Hanlon. We're not too sure of you . . . yet . . . because you were a cadet. Oh, we know," as Hanlon started to protest hotly, "all about your being kicked out. We can see how all that might well have soured you enough so you will really do anything you can to get ahead, even if only to show the Corps. But you can understand our hesitation, I think."

"Of course, sir. But you needn't worry." He made his voice as bitter and hard as he could. "I've had my fill of all that law and order stuff. I was an innocent young punk, full of high ideals and the romance of the Corps and all that bunk. But those mangy slime-snakes knocked all that out of me. Anything I can do that'll give 'em a kick in the teeth I'll do with joy and gusto!"

"Fine words," snapped the leader, "but can you take it if the going gets tough?"

Hanlon was learning fast. Now he stared straight back into those hard eyes.

"Can you dish it out, Mister?" his tone was almost, but not quite, insolent.

# Chapter 11

A BLACK LOOK SUFFUSED THE LEADER'S FACE AT Hanlon's impertinent "can you dish it out, Mister?" He half-rose from his seat, while the other four men reached quick hands towards their weapons.

Then slowly the man sank back, relaxed, and smiled—an open, friendly smile of genuine cordiality, and his men also relaxed.

"You'll do, Hanlon, by the great . . . uh . . . Zeus, you'll do! But," he added significantly, "I think you will find that I can 'dish it out', as you call it, if the need ever arises. You had better pray it never does."

"Fair enough," Hanlon shrugged indifferently.

"The boys will take you out and show you the town, if you like," the leader smiled engagingly. "They will get word to you when I have a job ready, which may be in a day or two."

Hanlon thanked him, and felt it policy to go out with "the boys," even though he did not particularly care to do so. Nor did he especially enjoy the night that followed.

He had left a ten o'clock call with the hotel's visiphone operator when he got back to the hotel at last. When she called he groggily opened one eye half way, and fumbled for the toggle-switch.

"H'lo."

"Ten o'clock of a fine morning, Mr. Hanlon."

"Oh, no!" he groaned.

"Oh, yes," she giggled. "That bad, is it?"

"Worse'n that. But thanks anyway . . . I guess."

She was laughing heartily as she disconnected.

Hanlon groaned with the utter misery of a hugely-distorted, throbbing head. The sunlight pouring through an open window directly into his eyes did not help any. He rolled over petulantly, but knew he had to get up.

He stumbled out of bed and went in to stand under a cold shower. Ten minutes later he began to feel a little more human, and decided maybe he would live after all.

"Never again!" he swore fervently. "I'm just not cut out for serious drinking. Hope I didn't give anything away to those guys last night."

He dressed slowly, meanwhile striving as best his aching head would let him, to review his situation. He was fairly well pleased with his success to date, but the grue of fear was still with him. He was getting part way where he wanted to be, but . . . this was certainly no picnic he was muscling into. He remembered his father's injunction to take it easy at first, and grimaced wrily.

Eating breakfast in the hotel dining room, after taking an effervescent to relieve his headache, he tried to plan his next moves. There wasn't much he could do, he decided, until they called him. He had made his bid—it wouldn't do to try to push himself too much, or it would look mighty fishy to those sharp minds.

He shuddered again, involuntarily, thinking about that enigmatic leader. Who . . . or what . . . was he?

Hanlon went first to the bank, and made out a card for his own box. But once in the vault, and the attendant gone out, it was box 1044 he opened. There was a note for him.

"Welcome to Simonides," he read. "My name—here—is Art Georgopoulis. I work at present as a bartender at the Golden Web, on Thermopylae street. The high-ups in the underworld hang out there, and I pick up occasional bits of news. If you come in, introduce yourself by asking for 'a good old Kentucky mint-julep,' Practically no one ever asks for those. I'm the blond, skinny one at the far end of the bar. If I can be of any help, just yell. Me, I haven't got to first check station yet—but I'm still in there punching. Hope you do better—Curt Hooper."

Hanlon "ate" the note, then wrote one of his own, telling what he had learned to date, what he suspicioned, and what he was trying to do. Of his new mental powers he said nothing. He did not distrust this SS man, of course, but if the fellow didn't know he couldn't be made to tell.

As Hanlon left the bank he began to get the feeling he was being trailed, but could not seem to locate anyone doing it, although he did not dare search to his rear very carefully. Neither could he catch any definite thoughts about such a thing from among the welter of thought-sensations on the crowded streets.

He wandered about most of the day, frankly sight-seeing—but his mind was always open. He went into various public buildings, sat for some time in one or another of the numerous parks whenever he felt a bit tired of walking.

That feeling of being watched made him cautious, so he did not practice much with his mind-control on any of the pigeon-like birds. He did, however, make a trip to the local zoo, and as he paused momentarily in front of each of the cages to look at the exhibit it contained, he briefly made an excursion into the mind of each different type of animal, bird or rodent. Outside of minor differences of texture, they all seemed about the same. Each of them had, naturally, different muscular abilities that would need considerable study if he ever intended using one of them.

And every minute he was seeking, searching for any tiniest thread of evidence as to what it was that was causing this undercurrent of secret intrigue that was so plainly evident to his super-sensitive mind.

But there was no factual data to be learned. Only that "feel" of it in the very air. Yet as the day wore on he came to believe that much or most of what he sensed was not that plot which was causing the Corps concern. Rather, it seemed more as though all the people here were engaged in some sort of secret aggressiveness.

And it was finally forced into his consciousness that it was "business," not "politics." For it was well-known that Simonides, even though it had become the Federation's wealthiest world, was not yet satisfied . . . that its merchants and traders wanted to capture more and still more of the System's business.

There were far too many minds engaged in aggressive thoughts for a political revolution, he felt sure. If it was this wide-spread, surely others of the Corps of the Secret Service would have found out something definite about it. No, whatever this was, it distinctly was not what he was here to find.

The feeling that he was being spied upon was always more or less present, but he could not spot the man or men who were watching him. Either several were working in short shifts, or else the trailer kept so far behind him that the multiplicity of thoughts from the hundreds of people always around masked those of the spy.

Hanlon ate a leisurely lunch in a small restaurant, and during the afternoon continued his apparently-aimless sight-seeing. If they were shadowing him, they would have nothing to report, he grinned. Not during the day, at least. What the evening would bring forth would perhaps be another matter.

For he had determined to at least get in touch with the SS man who had written that note. He would have dinner at the Golden Web, if they served meals. If not, he would have a drink anyway. The two men certainly should know each other by sight.

He went briefly to the hotel, but there had been no calls for him. So he took a ground-cab to the cafe, which turned out to be a pretentious, garish one. Inside he made his way to that part of the long, busy bar presided over by a slim, blond man.

Hanlon climbed onto a stool. "Gimme a good old Kentucky mint-julep, suh," he demanded, "an' be doggoned suah it's made right."

The bartender eyed him peculiarly. "Where's this Kentucky and what's a mint-julep?"

"On Terra, of course, where I came from. Where'd you think it was, on Andromeda Seven?"

"Pardon me, sir. I seem to remember now, having heard of such a drink. I'll have to look it up in the recipe-book— I disremember the ingredients."

Hanlon grinned and lost his appearance of truculence. "It's partly made of Blue Grass, like a 'horse's neck.' But if it's too much trouble, just give me a Cola."

The barkeep grinned, too. "I gotcha, Steve," and poured out the soft drink.

Hanlon sat sipping his innocuous drink, looking about him quietly. A large-sized crowd was beginning to fill the place—well-dressed, evidently fairly prosperous people, but he could see that they were not the real upper-class, but the slightly-off-shade climbers.

His drink finished Hanlon signalled his friendly barman. "The grub here any good? This looks like a nice place."

"Yes, it is. One often hears some interesting things here. As for the food, it is very good, and not too expensive. They have a native fowl much iike chicken I think you'd like. Ask for *poyka*, in whatever style you like it fixed. Glad to be of service, sir, any time, in any way." The last words were slightly emphasized.

Hanlon had ordered and was waiting for his food when a man he had never seen before slipped into the seat opposite him.

"The Boss wants to see you."

"Yeah?" Hanlon looked him up and down almost contemptuously. "Just who is this 'boss' who's interested in me?"

"Cut the clowning. You know who. At the Bacchus. Now!"

"So." Hanlon let himself appear slightly interested. "Well, after I get through eating, if nothing else shows up to interest me more, I might drop over."

"You'd better, and mighty quick, too!" the man snapped, although it was apparent he was puzzled by Hanlon's manner. "He don't like to be kept waiting."

"And I don't like to be hurried—or ordered about!" Hanlon snapped back. "If I come, and notice I said 'if,' I'll be there in about an hour. Now, do you mind? I like to enjoy my food."

The man rose, still with that perplexed expression. It was evident he was not used to people not jumping when his "Boss" issued invitations—which were really commands. He shook his head slowly. "I hope for your sake he's in a good humor," he said as he left.

Hanlon's mind was not too easy as he ate swiftly, and his relish of the excellent food was not as keen as it might have been but for this interruption. He shivered, remembering that cold ruthlessness he had sensed behind that leader's suave manner. But he had to play out his string as a somewhat brash youngster who wasn't afraid of anybody or anything. He had made a clean score with that reckless "can you dish it out, Mister?," but he had better not press his luck too far.

Thus it was only about half an hour later when he presented himself at the Bacchus.

"You took your time coming," the leader looked at Hanlon curiously.

"I was hungry," Hanlon answered simply. "I'd just ordered dinner when your message was delivered. I came as soon as I'd finished."

"Those who work for me usually . . . uh . . . come running when I call."

Hanlon grinned wolfishly. "Maybe they're afraid of you."

"And you aren't?"

"Should I be?"

"I don't like impudence or insolence," the voice was more curt and the eyes lost some of their calmness in a flash of anger.

Hanlon knew he had gone far enough for the time being, so instantly became less brash, more apologetic.

"If I take your job if you offer me one, sir, I'll obey all orders promptly, and I'll give you everything I've got, naturally. But I'm not one of your snivelling toadies."

The leader regarded him once more with silent appraisal, in which a measure of respect, or at least approval, seemed to show. Hanlon, probing the other minds present, was secretly amused at their astonishment at his temerity . . . and the fact that he was getting away with it.

Afer long moments the leader nodded his head, as though he had reached a decision.

"What were you doing in the bank this morning?"

"Why, just depositing some of my stuff in a safety deposit box," he said, surprised. "Why?"

"How did you get your own box so quickly?"

"What do you mean so quickly? I went in yesterday and asked if one was available, and the girl clerk signed me up for it, and said I could get entry today."

"Oh, I see. I was told it was done like you already had a box and . . . uh . . . wondered about it."

Hanlon reached in his pocket and threw a key onto the desk "Go look in it for yourself if you think it's important. And incidentally," he said contemptuously, "I've known all day long I was being shadowed." But was instantly sorry he had said that last.

For there came a deadly coldness in the leader's tone, and a gleam in those hard eyes that boded ill for someone. "I see. Well, let it pass." He pushed the key back toward Hanlon, who pocketed it thankfully. His bluff had worked. This was the key to his own box, of course; his master key was in a hidden pocket in the cuff of his trousers.

The leader sank back into his chair and was silent for long minutes, thinking deeply, while Hanlon waited patiently, still trying to get some glimmering of thought from that unreadable mind, still frustrated almost to the point of despair that he couldn't.

Finally the man spoke, but not to Hanlon. "Panek, you and the others go find Rellos and bring him here."

When they were alone, the leader leaned forward and spoke earnestly to Hanlon, yet watching him carefully as he did so. "i like you, Hanlon, and I'm going to test you out. I am not too sure of you, yet, but if I become so, you can go far—very, very far with me. This Rellos I sent for is the man who was shadowing you today. I cannot—*I will not!*" he spat venomously, "abide failure or incompetence. I am assigning you the pleasant little task of seeing that some sort of an . . . uh . . . accident happens to Rellos. And as I think about it, it might as well be a . . . uh . . . permanent one."

Hanlon's stomach curled up so tightly it hurt, but he strove manfully not to let his feelings show in his face. He'd had an instant's inkling of what the proposal was going to be, and it was a measure of his stability that he succeeded in keeping his mask up.

He knew starkly that this time he would have to go through with a killing, or else give up this line of research. For he knew that if he did not kill this man, this way was closed to him. And if he dropped out, but gave the tip to some other SS man, that one would eventually face the same sort of a task. So, much as it sickened him even to contemplate it, it now became a *must!* He would have to think of himself as a soldier in war, and Rellos an enemy.

Outwardly calm, he shrugged indifferently. "Any guy that can't produce isn't worth keeping," he said. "Any special way you want it done?"

"No . . . I think I would like to see how you work. Plan it yourself. But if it isn't done, you had better not let me or my men see you again."

"Fair enough. If I can't do a simple job like that I sure can't be of enough value to you to do myself any real good."

They were silent again, but Hanlon's mind was bleak with what was to come. He wasn't the killer type—he believed in the sacredness of human life. Yet he knew he would have to steel himself to go through with it. The job was more important than one man's life. But to kill in cold blood—a deliberate, planned-out murder!

Just then Panek returned with a slender, middle-aged man.

"Ah, Rellos," the leader greeted him. "I want you to meet a new member of our group, George Hanlon. He has just come from Terra, and has never been on Simonides before. I would like you to take him out and show him

New Athens and what it contains in the way of pleasures. You can turn in an account of your expenses tomorrow."

And *that*, thought Hanlon, was just about as low and slimy a trick as he had ever heard, and the thought came and would not be denied, that if it was this leader he was to kill he could do it cheerfully and with a clear conscience.

He rose, though, and smiled as he held out his hand. "Glad to know you, Rellos. It'll be fun comparing your amusements with those of Terra."

The man was somewhat sullen, although it was plain he did not dare show it too much before their boss. Hanlon could read enough from the new man's mind to know how deathly afraid he was of the leader, and how he hated him.

"Wonder why he's in this, feeling that way?" Hanlon thought swiftly, and during the evening tried to find out, but without success—the man steered clear of any such thoughts.

As the two went outside, the Simonidean asked curtly, "Wine, women or song?"

"Why not some of all three?" Hanlon laughed lightly. "Anything you think would be a lively evening, and that you'd enjoy."

The other unbent a little. "We'll go to the Phobos first, then. They have good liquor and a nice floor show. Good looking wenches who don't wear too much."

He hailed a ground-cab, which the two entered.

Hanlon couldn't enjoy that evening. In the first place, he couldn't ditch all his drinks—and he hated alcohol—yet had to remain as sober as possible. Second, and most disturbing, was that horrible thing he had to do, and he knew it must be carefully planned. A gun, knife or poison couldn't be used now—it must look so much like an accident that no possible blame could be attached to him; so that the police could not hold him even for a short time.

He thought of and discarded one plan after another, then remembered something seen during his wanderings— a pedestrian bridge crossing a high-speed truckway where the inter-city freighters were so numerous they ran almost bumper to bumper. "I'll lead him up there, then throw him over and down. He's sure to be run over and killed."

The nakedness of the girls at the Phobos, the coarse jokes of the so-called comedians, the raucous, ribald laughter of the drunken patrons disgusted Hanlon, and he was glad when they left.

"Let's walk a bit and see the sights," he suggested, and Rellos agreed after some argument—he wanted to visit more night clubs.

They had walked a couple of blocks along a residential street when a little, roly-poly puppy waddled out onto the sidewalk to greet them.

"What a cute . . ." Hanlon began, but with an oath, Rellos savagely and viciously kicked the little mite, sending it howling with pain across the low hedge.

A growl of anguish broke out, and Hanlon sent his mind searching for that deeper note. He found it, the mother dog, and was instantly inside that mind, controlling it.

With a leap the huge shepherd was over the hedge, straight at Rellos. The dog's weight bore the man backward, fighting for his life, trying to hold back those gleaming fangs straining for his throat.

Hanlon threw himself into the melee, but while ostensibly trying to drag the dog away, delayed the few seconds it took for those slashing fangs to rip out Rellos' throat.

People came running up, and as the first reached the spot they saw Hanlon struggling to hold back the snarling, blood-flecked dog, while Rellos lay dead in a pool of blood.

The dog's owner rushed up and snapped a leash on the dog.

"I'm terribly sorry, sir," Hanlon said. "My companion was drunk and kicked her puppy. She merely avenged it."

"I wondered," the man was shaken. "Kaiserina never was vicious before."

"I don't think she will be again," Hanlon said soothingly. "Is the puppy all right?" he asked the small boy who came up with the little animal cradled in his arms.

"No," the boy sobbed, "Fluffy's dead."

"What's going on here?" an authoritative voice said, and two policemen pushed their way through the quickly-gathered crowd.

The dog's owner explained in swift words, and completely exonerated Hanlon. "This man tried to stop my dog; he was holding her back when I got here," and others corroborated his statement.

"You'd better have the dog killed," the policeman said, but Hanlon intervened.

"No, she was just striking back at the man who killed her puppy. She wasn't to blame, and I'm sure she isn't vicious."

The police were finally satisfied, and while they were calling the dead-wagon Hanlon walked slowly back to his hotel, his heart still sick but consoled a bit.

"He had it coming to him," his thought was bitter. "The rotten beast—kicking a little puppy like that!"

# Chapter 12

THE NEXT EVENING HANLON WENT BACK TO THE Bacchus. Instead of stopping at the bar he went directly to the back room and knocked on the door.

When the peephole opened he asked, "The Boss in?"

"Nope."

"I've got a report to make."

"Wait at the bar. I'll get in touch."

A quarter hour later the man summoned him, and upon entering that now-familiar room Hanlon saw a closet door was standing open, disclosing a visiphone screen, on which the leader's face was visible.

"Well?"

"Yep."

"Ah!" There was a quick intake of breath, and a feral gleam in those greenish eyes. A moment's silence, then "Do you still want that overseer's job?"

"For a thousand a month and keep? Definitely!"

"Very well, we'll try you. Zeller will give you a list of things you'll need there—special clothing and such. Uh . . . got any money to buy those you don't have?"

"I will have when you pay me Rellos' expense money for last night."

The leader's eyes narrowed in sudden anger. "Don't try my patience too far, Hanlon."

"Okay," Hanlon shrugged indifferently. "But I never figured you for a cheapskate."

There was a gasp, as though the leader was amazed at Hanlon's temerity. But he quickly gained control of himself, and an instant later began smiling, then grinning and finally laughing aloud . . . at himself.

"By Zeus, Hanlon, I like you! Nobody else ever dared talk up to me like that. You win. Tell Zeller . . . no, put him on, I'll tell him . . . Zeller, give Hanlon the list of things needed for the mine-guard job, and pay him a hundred credits, charged to the 'accident fund'. Tell him to be here, all packed to go, at thirteen o'clock." He started to turn the set off, then, as he heard Hanlon ask "Anything else now?" faced the screen again.

"Not unless you want to make rounds with the boys again. It will be some time before you can have any night-life."

Hanlon made a sign of distaste and shook his head. "Unh-uh, thanks. Two big-heads in a row will last me for plenty time. I'll go get some shut-eye."

The leader smiled companionably. "The rest might be best, for you'll have a rather rough trip. You'll ride a freighter, not a luxury liner."

"Do I ask where I'm going?"

"Does it matter?"

Hanlon shrugged. "Not especially. Just curiosity."

"Then it won't particularly bother you if we . . . uh . . . keep your destination a secret for a while?"

"Not in the least, if you want it that way," he yawned indifferently. But his mind was so anxious he had trouble not letting it show in his face or eyes. How was he to get that location? He thought swiftly, and conceived a possibility.

"Your bar here serve Cola?"

"What is that?"

"A soft drink very popular on Terra and many other planets. I'd like to take a case with me, if it's allowed."

"I see no reason against it. I never heard of it, but you might ask the bargirls."

"I can get it at the Golden Web if you don't have it here. I had some there the other night."

He watched carefully but there was no sign of suspicion; the leader did not even seem interested.

Hanlon blanked the screen, got the list and money from Zeller, and walked out. The Bacchus did not stock Cola, so he took a ground-cab to the Golden Web.

Pretending half-drunkenness, he walked in and ordered the case of drink from his colleague. While drinking a glass of it, he talked in more or less garrulous tones. In between unimportant words he informed the SS man bartender that he was leaving the next noon for another planet whose name and location he hadn't yet been able to learn.

"Got a good boss, though," he mumbled thickly. "Very good boss—sure he knows a lot. Headquarters at the Bacchus."

Hooper, quick of understanding as all SS men have to be, merely said aloud the conventional "Safe Flights," but Hanlon knew he would do everything he could to get that planetary information.

And Hanlon was well content as he went to the hotel and to bed. What could be done, had been done.

As soon as he had breakfasted the next morning, Hanlon checked out of his hotel, then went out and purchased the special clothing and other items on his list. With everything packed in traveling cases, he presented himself at the Bacchus just before thirteen o'clock.

As he got out of the cab, and gave orders to the doorman about keeping his luggage until he was ready to leave, Hanlon was heartened to see Hooper, apparently reading a newsheet, leaning against the terrace-facade nearby.

In the back room the leader and three others, including the ubiquitous Panek, were waiting for him. He was handed an envelope.

"When you arrive, give these credentials to Peter Philander, the superintendent. He will be your boss there. Just do as he says, don't get nosey about what is going on, and you will do all right."

"Don't worry about my keeping my nose clean. I'm taking along a dozen extra hankies."

His last doubts about leaving Simonides to go to the unknown planet were now at rest. He was sure that there he would find the leads he so desperately needed—and probably only there could he get them.

They picked up his luggage, then all got into a large, black ground-car, and as it started the men lowered curtains over the windows. And while Hanlon was wondering about that, one of them pinned his arms suddenly to his side while another slapped a piece of adhesive across his eyes, smoothing it tightly into place.

Hanlon gasped, but did not struggle.

"That's right, don't fight it," the leader's voice was almost kind. "We just don't want you knowing where we are going . . . yet."

The car travelled some miles, then stopped and they all got out. The men helped Hanlon down, led him a few dozen steps, then helped him climb into another machine. In a moment he realized they were now in an aircar that had taken off, and he frowned. Assuming that Hooper had followed, he'd be out of it now. He was on his own.

For several moments Hanlon tried in vain to read from the others' minds where they were going. He had almost given up hope when he heard the unmistakable panting of a small dog, and realized that one of the air crew must have brought a pet.

Quickly his mind contacted that of the dog, and instantly was inside it, looking out through the dog's eyes. He controlled its mind so that it climbed up in the man's lap and, with its forepaws on the fellow's shoulder, looked out of the aircar's window. No one seemed to find anything peculiar in the dog's actions, its owner merely patting it as it stood there, as Hanlon could feel through the dog's senses.

Now Hanlon could see they were nearing some mountains, and took particular notice of everything that might be remembered as a landmark. Soon they were settling down into a little hidden valley, where there was a fairly large space-freighter.

They led him into this ship, and he lost the dog, so could not see just where they were taking him. Finally he sensed they were in a small room, and the adhesive was ripped from his face.

The leader and Panek stood in the small cabin with Hanlon.

"This is to be your cabin. Sorry for the precautions, but you can see why, I am sure. But if you behave, and make a good record, you won't have to . . . uh . . . worry about them any more. Take-off almost immediately, so we have to leave. Safe flights, and I hope you make out all right."

He looked fixedly at Hanlon for a long, long minute, and the young man, returned his gaze as steadily.

"I'll do my job," Hanlon said honestly after that moment—but it was his job for the Secret Service he meant. "Good-bye, and thanks. Thank you, too, Panek, for your help."

"Glad to've done it, Pal, glad to."

"See you in four months, then," and the two left.

Hanlon stored his luggage in the racks made for it, then started to go outside and see what was going on. But the door was locked.

"They sure don't want me to know where we're going," he grinned ruefully as he sat down on the edge of his bunk. "That makes me know it's important, and I'll get it some day—they can't keep it from me forever."

Sirens screamed "take-off," and he strapped himself into his bunk. When he felt the pressure subside and knew they were in space he unstrapped and relaxed. But there was nothing he could do.

Later there was the sound of a key in the lock. When the door opened a heavy-set man carrying a blaster stepped inside.

"Stand back, Bud, and keep your hands in sight."

Hanlon raised his hands while the messcook brought in a tray and set it on his bunk. As they were going out Hanlon spoke. "You got any books on board? I don't mind being locked in and won't make any trouble, but please give me something to do."

They made no answer, but when they returned for the empty dishes they left a couple of dog-eared magazines.

Late the following afternoon the siren warned of landing, and Hanlon strapped himself down again. After he had felt the landing, one of the ship's officers came and unlocked the door.

He was very apologetic. "Sorry, sir, about this, but we had our orders."

"It's okay with me," Hanlon said cheerfully. "Don't make a bit of difference with me where I am, long's I get well paid."

"I see you've put on your light clothing. That's good—this is a hot planet. These your bags?"

Hanlon nodded, and each carrying one, the officer led the way to the airlock and they climbed down onto this new world.

The air was thick and muggy—at least 110° Fahrenheit, Hanlon guessed. There was a great bustle of activity on the landing field. Automatic machinery was unloading cargo, and loading it into trucks. There were several men, with their luggage, standing about.

One was a huge, brutish-looking man, another a slender young chap about Hanlon's own age, apparently well-educated, from his manner, but with a certain shiftiness in his eyes; the others common-place laborers.

"Any of you been here before?" the officer asked.

Two of the others nodded, and started away from the field. Hanlon saw that just beyond the edge of it there were heavy forests—almost a jungle, but strange and alien.

As they drew nearer and finally entered it, the young SS man saw that this was, indeed, unlike any jungle or forest he had ever seen or heard about. Tall trees whose branches writhed as though alive, yet never attacked one. Underbrush so thick it seemed impassable, yet which twisted away from their approach as though afraid of a contaminating touch, only to swish back into place as soon as the men passed.

Hanlon, walking along and taking it all in, seemed to catch faint whispers of thought, but could make nothing of it. He wondered what it was—perhaps some alien animal-life very low in the scale?

The ground was soft and mucky. The young checker cautioned the others, "Don't step off the path; some of this stuff's almost like quicksand.

"There's a road to the mine," he answered Hanlon's further question, "but it's winding and about five miles, where this path's only a half mile. Ground here won't stand heavy loads."

"How big is this planet, anyway? Gravity seems about like Simonides and Terra."

"It's not quite as large, but seems composed mainly of heavier metals or something. Gravity about .93. The weather stays about the same all year 'round; very few storms of any kind, although there's a hot rain almost every night for about half an hour. The temperature goes down to about 90 at night; up to 110-115 days."

"No wonder they told me to buy light clothing."

"Yeah, it's sure hot. We'd go mostly naked, except the actinic's really fierce. Be sure to wear a hat all the time outdoors, and light gloves. If your eyes start to smart, wear dark goggles."

"Thanks for the tips, Chum, I appreciate 'em. I'd begun to notice skin itching, but thought it might be this jungle."

They broke through the final wall of foliage and Hanlon saw a large cleared space ahead that must have been roughly a half-mile across. There were quite a number of buildings, mostly windowless, and he decided they were storehouses.

"There's the messhall," his new-found friend pointed.

They went on to another long, low, bungalow-type building, inside which Hanlon saw a long hall from which opened dozens of doors on either side. The other men disappeared into one or another of the rooms, and the young fellow stopped at another door. "Grab the first room that has a key in the lock outside," he said. "They're all alike."

The SS man found one, with the number "17" on the door, and went in. The room was small but comfortably furnished. The bed had a good mattress, he found, and white linen sheets and a thin, fleecy blanket folded on the foot. There was a big easy chair, a closet for his clothes and a dresser with four drawers. Glo-lights were set in the ceiling, and there was another on a standard by the big chair for easy reading. A door opened into another room which proved to be a compact toilet and shower. Everything was immaculately clean, and the air was cooled and sweet from air-conditioning.

"Not bad, not bad at all," Hanlon said half-aloud as he unpacked and stored his things. Then he took a shower. "Man, are you going to get plenty of work-outs, in this heat," he apostrophised the shower, thankfully. Dressing again, he went out to locate Peter Philander, his new boss.

He stopped at the messhall, and there he found the cook, a jolly, roly-poly sort of man. He introduced himself and they chatted for a few minutes.

"I'm going to like this guy—hope they're all as nice and friendly," Hanlon thought. "Where's the super's office?" he asked, and the cook pointed it out.

Entering the office-shack, Hanlon found himself in a fairly large room with a number of desks and several drafting boards with blue-prints and drawings pinned on them. Behind one of the larger desks was a heavy-set man with a great, angry scar across his left check and neck, running from the bridge of the nose to below the ear.

Something about the man brought a sense of distrust to Hanlon—perhaps his looks, for that terrible scar made him look like a blood-thirsty pirate.

Hanlon discreetly let none of these things show in his voice or demeanor as he stepped forward, a smile on his face and his credentials in his hand. "Mr. Philander, sir? I'm George Hanlon, a new guard."

The other nodded without a word, and snatched at the papers, glaring at Hanlon in a squinting, suspicious manner.

Hanlon probed toward the mind behind that frown, and could sense a feeling of fear, suspicion and unrest. He caught a fragment of thought—"another one after my job?"—and in a flash of inspiration guessed what was wrong. This superintendent must have a terrible inferiority complex, which that disfiguring scar certainly didn't help. He was undoubtedly competent, or he would not be here, but felt every new man was a possible challenge or replacement.

Knowing that his papers made no mention of his having been a cadet, Hanlon took a chance on a course of action. "Gee, Mr. Philander, sir, I envy you," he said the moment the man looked up. "Knowing all about metals and ores and mining and stuff like that. I sure wish I'd had the chance to learn something valuable like that. But me, I guess I'm just a 'strong back; weak mind' sort of guy."

The superintendent looked at him piercingly for a long moment, as though trying to decide whether this was genuine or subtle sarcasm. He must have decided it was the former, for he relaxed a bit. "Yeah," he growled in a deep bass that seemed meant to be pleasant now. "It takes a lot of study and a good mind to learn what I know. Very few men can make the grade."

And Hanlon, who was by necessity swiftly becoming a good judge of character, knew he had this man pegged, and that while he would be dangerous if crossed, could be handled adroitly.

"Just what will my duties be, sir? Or have you delegated the handling of us guards to some lesser man?"

"No, I handle 'em myself. 'If you want a job well done, do it yourself', you know. I'll take you out and show you around. Are you all settled and comfortable?"

"Oh, yes, sir. I have a very nice room, number 17, and am all unpacked. Hunting your office I ran into the messhall, and Cookie told me about meal hours. I'm sure I'll get along fine here—as much as this awful heat'll let me. They sure weren't kidding when they said it was hot here. And I want to assure you, sir, that I'll work hard and tend strictly to business—nothing else."

The superintendent was becoming more mollified and less fearful by the second. Now he actually smiled, a rather pitiful travesty of a smile, and Hanlon's sympathy went out to him.

"Then we'll get along fine," Philander said. "Just remember that your job is only to keep the natives at work during your shift, and that in your off hours you do not go hunting 'round into things that're none of your business."

"Oh, naturally, sir. You just list what limits I'm to keep in, and I'll stay there. All I'm after here is that thousand credits a month, and as big a bonus as I can earn. You see," with engaging frankness, "I'm a guy that wants to make his pile as quick as possible, so I won't have to work all my life. I've got to work to get 'em, sure, but I don't aim to work forever."

"Hmmpff!" Philander rose from behind the desk. "Come on, I'll show you around."

# Chapter 13

**F**OR AN HOUR SUPERINTENDENT PHILANDER escorted George Hanlon about the diggings, showing him the various buildings and the workers' stockade. ("Prison" would be a better word, Hanlon thought, enraged that there were still men who would enslave others for their own personal gain.)

The young Earthman got a real shock of surprise at his first sight of the native. They were so entirely different from anything he had ever suspected might exist. They were tall and slender, and their greenish-brown skin was rough and irregular. They seemed possessed of considerable wiry strength, however.

Hanlon had the peculiar feeling that they were somehow familiar, as though related to something he already knew, even though they were so alien. But, strain as he might, he could not at first bring that illusive thought into recognition.

He examined more particularly each item of the natives' appearance. They had small triangular eyes, wide-spaced on their narrow faces, almost like a bird's yet not set quite as far back. They could see forward and somewhat to either side, he guessed, with a much wider range of vision than humans have. They also had triangular-shaped mouths which worked somewhat on the sphincter method. Even though their faces were sort of silly-looking, there was somehow a strange beauty to them.

He noticed that when two or more faced each other they often worked their mouths, and guessed they were conversing, although not a sound could be heard coming from them, other than a peculiar, faint rustling as they moved.

It was the latter that gave him the clue. *Animated*

*trees!* That's what they reminded him of. That skin of theirs was like new bark; their limbs were irregular, suggesting the branches of a tree, rather than the graceful roundness of human and Terran animal's limbs.

He turned excitedly to Philander. "Hey, those natives are partly vegetable, aren't they? Like trees that can move and think?"

"That's what they say," Philander said shortly, "though I don't know about the 'think' part No one's ever been able to figure 'em out They don't talk, and can't seem to hear us, no matter how loud we yell. We have to show 'em everything we want 'em to do, and give 'em orders by signs. Which don't do any good when they loaf—they don't seem to feel 'em So we use electric shock-rods, like you see that guard there carrying.

Hanlon was silent for several moments, but his mind was attempting to probe into that of the native nearest him. Nor was he surprised to discover that this native had a really respectable mind—alert and keen.

Hanlon could read quite easily pictures of various things —but he could not interpret them. Yet he could feel their sense of shame and degradation at such an enslaved condition, and the dull anger they felt for the humans who had made them so.

This promised to be a fertile field for study, and the young SS man felt a thrill that he could do a lot of prowling and studying without seeming to break the rules Philander had laid down for his conduct. "This certainly is my field," he thought. "I'm sure glad I decided to take the chance of coming here—the Corps must learn of this situation."

The superintendent broke in on his thoughts. "I've got to go back to the office before dinner. Go to the commissary store, there, and get your chronom exchanged for one that runs on Algonian time. Yours will be stored for safekeeping and changed back if or when you leave here."

As he walked away Hanlon thrilled to the knowledge that he had gained two valuable pieces of information.

First, and most important, the name of this planet— Algon. Second, but this one a bit dismaying, that there might be some doubt as to whether or not he would ever leave here. Was there some danger here of which he had not been told . . . or was it that the leader's promise of four months' work and then a vacation back to Simonides perhaps meant nothing at all—was merely a "come on"?

It was more than the perspiration from the terrible heat that dampened Hanlon's skin as he walked thoughtfully over to the store. Yet he tingled with the knowledge that at least he knew where he was. Now, his only worry was getting that knowledge to the Corps.

At dinner a little later he had his first chance to meet all the men with whom he would be working. The superintendent introduced them all around when they sat down at the long table.

There were eleven other guards, all older, all bigger men than he. They were alike in that all appeared to be swaggering bullies, and he could well imagine how ready they were with the use of those shock-rods, or other forms of brutality, to torture the Algonians at the least provocation or no provocation whatever. Without exception these guards had heavy faces, most of them unshaven, and most with thick, shaggy eyebrows. Even in that air-cooled room their generally unwashed condition was noticeable.

Hanlon knew instinctively he would make no friends among them. "I only hope I make no enemies. Why was I, so drastically different from them, chosen as a guard? What's that leader got in his devious mind, anyway?"

There were four mining engineers, and these men were keen, alert fellows. One seemed about forty-five, another in his late thirties, and the two others young men evidently not long out of school. They were clean-shaven, and friendly where the guards were surly and sneering at Hanlon's youth and slimness.

There was an accountant, the store clerk, two checkers who tallied ore brought up each shift. A half dozen others, who apparently were truckmen and hoistmen, completed, with Philander, the cook and the bunkhouse cleaner, the human crew at this mine.

Hanlon had been seated between one of the guards, a huge man by the name of Groton, and one of the young engineers. The latter made him welcome, and asked where he came from.

"I'd just moved to Simonides when I got the chance

to come here," Hanlon explained. "I was born and raised on Terra."

"Terra!" the young man's voice was interested, and several others about the table raised their heads at that name. "I've always wanted to see the Mother World."

When all had finished eating, several of the other men who had never seen Terra moved closer to Hanlon, asking many questions.

"I understand Terra has the best technicians in the universe," one of the hoistmen said.

"That used to be the case," Hanlon answered honestly, "but now I understand Simonides has, just as she is the wealthiest planet. Of course, Terra being the original world, was bound to have the best the race could breed in all lines of endeavor. But when so many people migrated to other planets, she gradually lost many of her finest brains. Later, those other planets offered such fabulous wages to men and women with skills and trainings her first inhabitants lacked, that Terra was further drained."

"That's the pity of colonization," the elder engineer sighed. "It builds new lands at the expense of the old, taking all their strongest, most adventurous and most imaginative. Soon the original country or continent or planet is peopled only by the dregs."

"I don't like to think Terra has only dregs left. After all, I came from there, you know," Hanlon grinned and they smiled back companionably. "But I know you're right in part—at least, that will probably be the case in time. Just as it will with the other planets as their best and younger top-notchers go out to open up still more worlds."

In the middle of that first night on Algon something, perhaps his sub-conscious, brought George Hanlon wide awake, his every mental faculty clear and alert.

*Click! Click! Click!* . . . like pieces of a jig-saw puzzle falling into place, many of the odds and ends of apparently unrelated information and experience fell into place in this enigma.

He remembered clearly now, an incident that had merely brought a momentary wonder at the time. Those last minutes before the ship took off. The leader had stared long and piercingly into his eyes and Hanlon, wondering and puzzled as to what the man was seeking, merely stared back dumbly. Now he remembered the flashing thought —quickly dismissed as ridiculous—that even if he did find out where he was going, he must never tell anyone; must forget it entirely and instantly on pain of severe torture.

Why, that leader must have been trying to implant a hypnotic compulsion in his mind . . . and must have thought he succeeded, else Hanlon would never have reached here alive. *That* was why he could never read that knowledge from the mind of any of the people he had contacted who were in on this game—not even that ship's officer, who certainly should have known.

But wait a minute. What about Philander? He knew. Hadn't the hypnosis worked on him? Or was that name "Algon" merely one the super used in place of the real one he didn't know he knew? Or, again, could it be that he was so well trusted that the knowledge had not been sealed off from him?

Of the three, Hanlon argued the latter was probably the truth.

Another point. That vague reference to "if or when you leave here" was undoubtedly a slip of the tongue. Philander had probably guessed—or perhaps it was so with all first-time men—that Hanlon was here on probation. "If so," the thought was insistent, "I sure will have to watch my step every minute, and not let slip what I'm trying to do here." But further moments of thought brought the reasonable conclusion that he could lull their suspicion by buckling down and making a real record for efficiency.

Or . . . and this gave him the cold shivers for a moment, so that he instinctively burrowed a bit further down beneath the sheet, as though it could protect and warm him . . . did they know all about him already, and had sent him here to get rid of him? Was he to become another victim of one of the leader's "little accidents"?

Yes, if they still disbelieved his story about his dismissal, they might well be determined to get rid of him in a way that would not incriminate them. They would know that if Hanlon was still a Corpsman his death would be most thoroughly investigated.

Perhaps . . . but if that was the case, why let him get here at all? His "accident"—fatal, of course (so sorry!)—

could just as well have occurred on the way. No, more likely he was still on probation. They were not quite sure of him, but were giving him the benefit of the doubt. The leader seemed to like him, in a curious way.

Well, he was now warned, and would watch himself more carefully than ever . . . and he had learned a lot, and would learn more. He smiled contentedly and went back to sleep.

The next day he had his first taste of guarding the natives as they worked. The superintendent himself inducted him into the task.

Shortly before shift time, Philander appeared at Hanlon's room just as the young man was putting on the special clothing he had been told to wear on duty in the mine.

"Ready?" Philander was strangely courteous and cooperative. "Let's go collect your crew."

They went over to the stockade, the superintendent giving Hanlon a key as they unlocked the gates. Hanlon saw that the corral was divided into twelve sections.

"One guard has charge of all the natives in one section, and they all work each shift," Philander explained.

"What if one of them is sick?"

"They don't get sick," the man's voice was gruff, and Hanlon's first thought was that what he really meant was that the natives were worked no matter how they felt. But he quickly became ashamed of the thought—he didn't know anything about them yet, and perhaps they actually never did get sick. He would have to quit jumping to conclusions that way—it would seriously retard his ability to make correct deductions.

At the rearmost section, Philander opened another gate with the same key, and flashed his portable glo-light inside the large hut that covered most of the space of the section. Hanlon, close behind, could see about twenty of the "Greenies," as he had learned they were usually called, standing or lying about. There was no furniture inside, no chairs nor stools, tables or beds.

"They eat and sleep standing up—that's why the huts don't need any furnishings," Philander explained.

At sight of the men and the light, most of the natives

began moving toward the door. A few at the back didn't move fast enough to satisfy Philander, and with a curse he ran back and touched them with that shock-rod he carried.

Hanlon could see an expression of agony on the faces of those touched, and as they writhed away from the rod he realized it must be very painful, indeed, if not exquisite torture to them. They now jumped forward, and huddled pathetically near the door.

Philander took a long, light but very tough line from his pocket. It had a series of running nooses in it, and he slipped one of these about the wrist of each native, drawing it tight. Then he half-led, half-dragged them out of the stockade, to the mine entrace, and down the drift to the rise they had to climb to get to the stope Hanlon's crew was to work.

Once there, and released from the rope, the natives seemed to know what they were supposed to do, and sullenly started doing it.

"You usually use three pickmen, four shovellers, four for your timbering crew, three sorters, and six on the wheelbarrows," Philander explained. "Sometimes, if the vein widens out enough, you get extra hands to work the wider face, but this size crew generally works out best. You'll soon get used to it so you'll know how many you need. If more, just yell and you'll get 'em. If it happens the vein narrows so you can't use all these to best advantage, someone working a wider vein can use your extras temporarily."

"I get it," Hanlon was very attentive. He was determined to learn this work quickly and thoroughly, and to make a good record.

Philander showed Hanlon the difference between the ore and the surrounding rock, and explained very carefully how he was to watch especially for any side veins branching off from the main one. "Make sure the Greenies clean out all the ore as they go along, before it's timbered up."

"I understand everything so far."

"Keep the lazy beggars going full speed," Philander was very emphatic. "Don't let 'em lag, or they'll wear you down. Don't ever let 'em get out of control, or put anything over on you, especially in sorting ore from rock.

They're tricky. Use your shock-rod at every least sign of mutiny or loafing. Make 'em respect you. They know better'n to try to get away, 'cause they hate the rod."

"What does it do to them?"

"We don't know exactly, except they can feel it, and will do anything to get away from it."

"Maybe it hurts them terribly."

"Look, punk!" Philander lost his friendliness, and snarled at Hanlon with twisted face. "We don't care whether they like it or not. They know their jobs and they don't have to get shocked if they keep working. So it's strictly up to them. Don't go getting any soft notions about these lousy Greenies. They're only dumb brutes fit for working—so work 'em!"

"I'll work 'em," Hanlon said.


# Chapter 14


YES, HANLON WOULD WORK THE NATIVES, but without cruelty. His thoughts were a seething of contempt for these brutal thugs. He was willing to bet, right there and then, without knowing anything about this situation, that these natives could be controlled without bullying or hurting them—and better.

Having had military training, Hanlon knew it was possible to enforce the most strict discipline without such means, and that any man . . . or entity, probably . . . could and would submit to discipline fairly and decently enforced, with far less trouble and animosity, and with far greater productivity than if he were driven to it.

"Anybody works better for a pat on the back than for a kick in the pants!" he thought indignantly.

Philander stood about for an hour, and when he saw that Hanlon understood exactly what was expected of him and his crew—when he saw Hanlon several times correct

the sorters who had left too much rock in with the ores—
he turned to leave.

"You'll hear the siren when the shift's over," he said.
"Bring your gang back and lock 'em in the stockade then.
Be sure you lock both gates carefully."

"Cookie gave me a lunch for half-time," Hanlon said.
"What about the natives? Do they eat then, too?"

"Naw, they don't eat," was the surprising answer.
"Once a day they stick their hands into the dirt for nearly
an hour. Must get nourishment that way."

"That seems to prove they're vegetable matter. Their
fingers must be some sort of feeding roots," Hanlon observed sagely. "They sure are the strangest beings I've ever
heard of."

The superintendent shrugged and left without further
words.

Hanlon looked about and found a rock near the sorters,
and used this for a seat. He sat watching the natives work,
and speculating about them, and also about what this was
all about. The mine seemed to him a very rich one, and
by using slave labor those men could well be reaping a
huge fortune from it. No wonder they could afford to
pay guards a thousand a month.

After a bit one of the natives, seeing Hanlon merely
sitting there instead of being alertly on guard close to
them, dropped its shovel and turned away from its work.
Hanlon got up leisurely, but walked purposefully over to
confront the Greenie. He smiled and motioned the native
back to work.

The Greenie's face showed surprise at Hanlon's action,
but it made no move to go. It did, however, appear to
be keeping its eyes alertly on that dread shock-rod hang-
ing loosely in Hanlon's hand. The guard could see that
the others had also stopped work, and were carefully watching the little drama.

Hanlon smiled and again motioned the native back to
work, and when it did not move, he reached out, grasped
it gently by the shoulder and, still gently, pushed it in the
direction of its shovel, with what was really a pat on the
back.

There were looks of surprise that amounted almost to
stupefaction on the faces of all the natives. The one who

had first stopped now picked up its shovel and resumed work, and the rest followed its example. Hanlon resumed his seat, still with that friendly smile on his face. He noticed with satisfaction that they were soon working harder and faster than before the incident.

"I was right," he told himself almost smugly.

The six hour shift was finally ended without any further show of resistance. That is, it was six hours by Algonian time, but about eight by Terra standards. For on Algon, while the day had been divided by the humans into twenty-four hours, the same as on Earth, each hour was almost seventy-eight minutes long. They divided the year into five day weeks, though, so it averaged out about the same.

When the siren blew Hanlon smiled happily at his crew as he herded them together, and made applauding motions with his hands, wondering if they understood what he meant.

When he had locked the natives in their stockade, he hunted up the checkers. "How'd I do?" he asked. "Come anywhere near what I was supposed to get out?"

One of the checkers totalled up his figures, then looked up in surprise. "Hey, kid, you did all right. Nearly a hundred pounds over the usual output, and clean, too. That's really okay for a new guard, and then some. Didn't have any trouble, eh?"

"Trouble?" Hanlon asked naively. "Was I supposed to have some?" Then he couldn't help grinning. "Thanks for the info," and went to his room, took a shower to cool off after that muggy heat in the mine, then tumbled onto his bunk for a nap until dinner-time.

Those first days so thoroughly disgusted George Hanlon as he saw the continued and senseless brutality the guards used toward their native "slaves," that he had trouble concealing his feelings. He continued to treat his Greenies with the respect he felt was due them, and he could not help but notice they seemed to look on him more and more as their friend. They always smiled when he looked at them, and before many days he discovered that his crew was doing more work than any of the others. His mind-probing had convinced him they were high enough in the scale of evolution to know the meaning of gratitude, and he could tell they were repaying his kindness with co-operation.

He had begun to make much more sense out of the pictures he saw in their minds, and to get some glimmerings of understanding about their alien concepts. Also, it was increasingly borne in upon him that they did "talk" to each other, and he guessed shrewdly that the reason no one could hear them was because their voices were above . . . or below? . . . the range of human hearing. "Above," he finally deduced.

That gave him the idea for an experiment, and he started whistling as loud as he could, gradually raising his tones until he was at the top of his range. He saw with interest and excitement that the last one or two shrillest notes seemed to attract their attention. Their silly-looking little triangular ears perked up and began twitching. They turned about, as though seeking the source of that sound, while every mouth began working with signs of utmost excitement, and his mind caught concepts of surprise and wonder.

That convinced him and so, in his next several off-hours, he surreptitiously collected various articles and pieces of material, and in his room started the construction of a little machine. His course in the Corps school had included considerable mechanics and electronics, and the tearing down and rebuilding of many of the machines and instruments the Corps used.

What he was trying to make now was a "frequency-transformer." If it would do what he was sure it would, and if he was right about the Algonians having vocal ability, they should be able to hear each other, and some day he might learn their language well enough to converse with them.

He finished it and smuggled the little box-like machine into his place in the mine. When he had his crew down there and working at their tasks, he got out the little box. He turned on the current from the small battery installed in it, then began talking at the same time he was turning a rheostat higher and higher. Finally he noticed those mobile ears began to twitch, and as he turned the tones higher and still higher, more and more of the natives stopped work and turned toward him. Finally he noticed an intenser excitement among them, and they dropped their tools and came crowding closer to him and his machine, their little eyes almost emitting sparks of excitement.

He thrilled with the realization that it worked. Now he turned another knob more and more, and gradually from the speaker came a jumble of sounds much like "mob-mutter," but very low. He kept on turning the rheostat until the incoming voices seemed about the same pitch as his own voice.

The excitement of the natives had grown to tremendous proportions, and his own equalled theirs. Their little mouths were working faster, and an expression almost like laughter came onto their peculiar little faces, as they heard his voice and knew he could now hear theirs.

Hanlon's own smile almost cracked his face. He realized he had learned something none of the greedy, power-mad Simonideans knew, and felt that here was the possible beginning for his campaign to free these poor native slaves.

He beckoned to one of the nearer natives to come to his side, then waved the rest back to their work. They looked at him questioningly for a moment, but he smiled reassuringly at them and they, having learned that he never used that dread shock-rod on them, all went back to their labors, leaving the one native standing there.

Hanlon looked earnestly at the Greenie, pointed a finger directly at himself and spoke into the microphone of his transformer. "Hanlon," he said slowly and distinctly, and repeated it a number of times, tapping himself on the chest each time he said it.

A smile of comprehension broke over the native's little face and he tapped himself the same way and said a word that came out of the speaker sounding like "Geck."

Hanlon reached out and touched the native and said "Geck." The Greenie in turn tapped Hanlon and said "An-yon," and they had made the first beginnings of understanding each other.

From then on this one native was released from all other work while Hanlon's crew was on duty, and the two devoted all their efforts to learning how to talk to each other.

Hanlon was pleased, but not especially surprised, to note that the rest of the crew—now almost entirely without his supervision—worked harder than ever, and that their daily output of ore grew progressively greater each shift, and all clean ore.

Hanlon's first exultant thought had been to run to Philander and tell him of what he had learned concerning the native's speech ability, and how he had made it possible for humans to talk to them.

But more sober reflections during that long work-shift brought caution. He decided this was a bit of knowledge he had better keep to himself as long as possible. He hoped he could keep it until he had learned how to talk with these people and learned much about, them, their situation, and how it could best be ameliorated.

The other men, he knew, considered the natives simply beasts, and would probably take away his transformer, instead of using it to learn about the Greenies as he planned to do.

By the end of a month he and Geck were chatting away like brothers. Each had learned enough of the other's language so that by using a mixture of the two they could exchange almost any thought concept desired. Hanlon's ability to read the native's surface thoughts helped a lot, especially as he began to understand their alien ways of thinking. Even so, he was surprised at how quickly Geck was picking up his own language.

Hanlon found that these people, while they had no scientific or mechanical knowledge or training of their own, did have highly developed ethical principles which governed all their individual and collective actions. They were a simple, natural people, with a native dignity Hanlon almost envied.

He found, too, that his first shrewd guess was correct—their bodies were of vegetable matter, rather than protoplasmic. They reproduced by budding, and he saw a number of the "females" to whom were attached buds of varying sizes. One day he watched interestedly while one of the ripened buds, a fully-developed individual but only about ten inches high, detached itself from its parent and dropped to the ground. It lay there for some minutes while the "mother" watched it carefully. Then it rose by

itself and trotted away with her as she resumed her work—
a miniature but fully alive native "child." It would take
about two years for it to attain its maturity, Geck informed
him. Hanlon asked, and Geck said it could take care of itself alone in the forest, so Hanlon managed to sneak it
out into the woods, where it would be free.

Geck told him that about four years previous a great
"egg" had landed here on Guddu, which was their name
for the planet. Men had come from inside it, and scattered
all about, seeking the metal ores they were now mining.

The natives, friendly and childishly curious, had gathered in force to watch these strange new creatures, and
because of their trusting natures had been easily trapped,
imprisoned and forced to work long, hard hours in the
rapidly-deepening holes.

"Us die swiftly away from sunlight," Geck said sadly.
"Us have very long life-span, but underground work make
us wither-die fast. Idea often discussed among we to dis-
continue race, because soon all we be gone anyway."

That quiet, hopeless statement made Hanlon madder
than a wet cat.

"What do the shock-rods do to you?" he asked after
a while.

"Affect we's nervous system some way. Us get most
terrible cramps. Is horrible agony. Us so thankful you
never use."

"I knew you would work without them as long as you
were treated fairly."

To himself Hanlon swore a determined oath to finish
this business entirely, some way or another. He realized
his limitations—one young, inexperienced man against
twenty ruthless, wealth-and-power greedy ruffians . . . and
that only here, at this one mine. No telling how many
others there were on Algon, besides all those back on
Simonides, and who knew what other planets, who were
in on this plot.

His heart clamored for swift action—his brain coun-
selled caution and careful planning.

# Chapter 15

**H**ANLON WAS SITTING AT HIS USUAL PLACE in the mine one day when one of the barrow-men ran up and spoke swiftly to Geck, who turned to Hanlon, alarm on his face. "Big boss man come."

Hanlon jumped to his feet. "Get everyone to work; tell them to act real busy!" he snapped. "You, too!"

He thrust the frequency-transformer into a hole prepared for just such an emergency, grabbed up his shock-rod and stepped closer to the natives. He was standing there, to all appearances strictly on the job of making his charges work, when Philander came crawling up the rise into the pocket where this crew was mining the glossy, lustrous pitch-blank uraninite ore.

"How're things going?" the superintendent greeted Hanlon with at least the appearance of friendliness.

"Just fine," the young man responded. "Everything's under control."

"Been looking over the reports, and see your crew is getting out more ore'n any of the others," the super's voice held just a tinge of anxiety, and Hanlon began probing that mind to see if he could discover just what all this portended.

"I just keep 'em at it," he shrugged.

"No trouble?"

"Nope, no trouble. Look at 'em," he waved his hand at the busy crew.

The big man regarded them closely, and could see that every single one of the natives was working at what he knew was their top speed, and without a single slacker. Even the barrow-men were moving almost at a jog-trot rather than the lazy saunter most natives used in an effort to do no more than they were forced to do.

Philander shook his head wonderingly. "How d'you do it?" he asked. "The other guards have to keep shocking one after another of the lazy dogs, yet you've made no move at a single one—and they keep right on hustling. I've never seen a crew work so hard."

Hanlon wanted desperately to tell him, but he decided the time was not yet. So he merely shrugged the question away as of little consequence. "I dunno, sir. I just stand around watching 'em, and they work." He grinned into the super's face. "Must be my manly charms—er sumpin'," he chuckled. Then sobered. "Maybe one reason is that I rotate 'em. Any job gets monotonous, so every hour or so I let 'em change around, from pick to barrow to sorting, and so on."

A frown of annoyance came onto Philander's face, but he quickly erased it. After all, this man was getting out more ore than the others, and that was what he was here for. How he did it didn't matter so much, after all, as long as he kept up his record.

But Hanlon, reading those surface thoughts, knew that the official was still very suspicious—and vastly worried. Hanlon knew he had to disarm the super some way, to get him out of that mood. He decided his air of naivete could still do the trick.

"Mr. Philander, sir," his voice was very ingenuous, "I don't want to pry into anything that's none of my business, but would you mind telling me what this stuff is we're getting here? It isn't anything dangerous, is it? I mean, it isn't one of those . . . those radium ores that make a fellow sterile, is it? I may want to get married some day, so I don't want to take any chances."

The mining engineer looked at him blankly for a moment, then threw back his head and his laughter rolled out until it seemed to fill the stope. Hanlon watched the other's mind clear itself of all suspicion . . . at least for the time being.

Philander rested his hand companionably on the younger man's shoulder. "No, it's nothing like that, so you can quit worrying. And the bonus you'll get, if you can keep up this output, will fix you so you can afford a wife when your time's up and you go back to Sime."

"Gee, that's good," Hanlon made his voice and face

show how relieved he felt. "It had me worried, even though I haven't got a girl yet."

The superintendent seemed in good humor now. Hanlon caught the thought that this punk was a good guard, and bright, and he did get the stuff out. The plan of rotating the workers was good—he'd order the other guards to use it. This Hanlon probably was no menace to their plans here, after all. In fact, maybe later they could use him on the bigger job. He (Philander) would so recommend to His Highness when he made his next report.

After a few more casual words the super left, and Hanlon sank back onto his favorite lounging place, thinking very seriously and contemplatively about this whole matter.

Again he had run into that thought about someone called "His Highness," but never any indication as to who the man was, or what position he occupied. It was now apparent that this individual was the man he would have to ferret out, whose plans he would have to learn before the Corps could take any really effective action.

He certainly hoped that one was the top man. It was going to be hard enough to get a line on him—to say nothing of anyone even higher.

One evening at dinner, some time later, Hanlon became aware that the guard, Gorton, was growling at him. He looked up in surprise, and forced himself to pay attention to the big man's words.

"I ask ya, whatcha tryin' t' do, punk?" the small pig-eyes glared redly at him, and the voice was harsh and bitter. "Try'n'a show up us other guards? What'sa big idea, gettin' out more ore'n we do?"

Hanlon stared back in amazement, and his voice when he answered was a stammer of surprise. "Why . . . why . . . I'm not trying to do anything . . . except my job," he added more forcefully.

"We been gettin' out a reg'lar three tons a shift," the ugly face was shoved closer to his, and Hanlon shrank back from the stench of raw spirits breathed on him. "What'sa idea drivin' yer crew up t' three an' a half er four?"

"I was told to keep my crew working, and I've been

doing that . . . and only that!" Hanlon snapped. "And take your ugly, stinking face away from mine!"

The disgust he felt at the brutality of these guards had made him so soul-sick with them he wasn't going to take any guff from one of them. Even though Gorton outweighed him by a good sixty pounds and probably had at least four inches longer reach, Hanlon wasn't afraid of him.

Right now he was as much in the mood for a fight as the guard seemed to be, for at Hanlon's words Gorton's huge, ham-like hand suddenly slapped out at the younger man. Hanlon wasn't able entirely to dodge safely, sitting as close as they were. His head rang from the terrific blow. He grabbed his cup of steaming coffee, and threw it backhand into Gorton's face.

Bellowing in pain and anger, the guard jumped up, upsetting the bench, and almost Hanlon with it. But the younger man was agile, and kept his feet. As Gorton rushed, his long, heavy arms flailing, Hanlon ducked away and jumped back far enough to get a firm footing on a cleared space of floor.

All Corps cadets were well-trained in both Marquis of Queensburg boxing, Judo and no-holds-barred barroom brawling. He knew all the questions . . . and all the answers.

So Hanlon stepped back in quickly. While Gorton was out of position from that abortive mighty swing, he drove his fist to the wrist into the big man's soft belly. As Gorton doubled up with an explosive grunt, Hanlon swung from the heels. His uppercut caught the big fellow flush on the jaw, and staggered him.

But Gorton could take it, and charged again, roaring curses. By sheer weight he bore Hanlon back across the floor, and got in a couple of heavy blows. Hanlon's right cheek was badly bruised, and that eye almost closed. But he was fighting methodically, almost viciously. He was in and out, slashing and ripping Gorton's face to shreds.

The other guards had been yelling their delight at the fight, and their hatred of the brash newcomer who was destroying their easy set-up. It was plain they were all on Gorton's side, and hoped to see Hanlon get thoroughly whipped.

"Bat his ears off, Gort!"

"Pound some sense inta him!"

"Show him who's top man aroun' here!"

One of them was not content with yelling. As Hanlon stepped to one side to avoid another of Gorton's rushes, this guard stuck out his leg and tripped Hanlon, who fell backward. Instantly Gorton was on him, and a great heavy-shod foot shot out in a kick that would have broken Hanlon's every rib. But the SS man was watching for just such tricks. His feet snaked out and hoisted Gorton so high and so far that when he landed he crashed like a great falling tree. Hanlon jumped to his feet and swung to confront his foe. But Gorton's head was bleeding badly, his eyes were closed, his face contorted. He was out like a burnt match.

Instantly Hanlon sank to his knees by the fallen man, gently raising the head and yelling for cold water and a towel. When the cook came running with them, Hanlon worked as swiftly to revive the guard as he would have done for his friend.

The other guards were so surprised at this act of mercy they sat like dull clods. But a couple of the engineers rose and came swiftly to help Hanlon. One of the checkers ran to Philander's office for the first aid kit.

The men were working desperately to stanch the flow of blood when Superintendent Philander came running in with the clerk and the kit. Taking in the situation at a glance, he demanded an explanation.

"Th' punk jumped Gort an' tried t' kill 'im!" one of the guards yelled, but was shouted down by the engineers, the checkers and the cook before the other slow-witted guards came to their senses enough to corroborate their fellow's mendacious claim.

The senior engineer explained fully and concisely what had actually happened. "Yet after all that, the kid was the first to help him, even though Gorton started the fight for no reason."

Just then the fallen guard groaned and began to regain his senses. The men helped him to his feet. He blinked for some moments, as though trying to figure out what had happened to him, then remembrance came.

"Why, that little squirt, hittin' me wit' a chair!" he

yelled, and struggled to get at Hanlon again, nor did the
men have an easy time holding him back.

Philander planted himself squarely in front of the angry
man. "Shut up!" he blazed, and the tone of command
halted the big fellow; he stared stupidly at his boss, as
though disbelieving his ears. "You keep your hands off
Hanlon!" the super emphasized his words by tapping
Gorton not gently on the chest. "I hear of any more of
this, and it's the jug 'til the next ship comes, then back
to Sime."

He whirled to face the table. "That goes for all the
rest of you rats, too! If Hanlon does his job better'n you,
it's 'cause he's a better man. Try to match him—don't
go gunning for him!"

"He your pet, Pete?" one asked mockingly.

"No, he's not my pet, Pete," the super's voice mimicked
the tone, although his face went red at the accusation.
"I just don't want this camp messed up with any feuds.
That'd cut down production, and the Big Boy wants this
ore out fast. If Hanlon can work his crew faster'n harder'n
the rest of you, you'd a blasted sight better find out how
he does it, not try to cut down his take. How'd you like
to go back to Sime and try explaining to His Highness
why you're not getting out as much stuff as's been proved
possible?"

That stopped them cold. Hanlon, watching their faces
and reading their minds, saw them shiver at thought of
having to face that feared individual—whoever he was.
They were more scared of him than of the Devil—that
was evident.

The men resumed their eating without another word—
that threat had cowed them as no amount of physical
chastisement or other punishment could possibly have
done. Philander set about sewing up and binding Gorton's
head-wound and his cut and bleeding face.

Hanlon resumed his own seat after washing up and
treating his own bruises with the cook's help. As he ate
he sought mind after mind in the vain endeavor to discover
any possible scrap of information about this enigmatic,
unknown Highness.

But he drew blank after blank, as far as definite data
was concerned—just as he had always done. The surface

thoughts of each man there showed plainly their fear of that implacably cold and vicious brain, but none of them held a picture of him.

They knew no excuses for failure were ever accepted. They knew terrible punishments were certain to follow when anyone was luckless enough to incur that monster's displeasure.

But Hanlon shivered, himself, as he saw how clearly those hardened criminals feared that mysterious man's displeasure. He quailed momentarily at thought of what would happen to him if he were caught trying to locate that man and his plot.

Hanlon knew a long moment of utter discouragement. There was so much he *had* to know before he could lead the Corps in clearing up this mess. There had been so many mentions of a "main plot" that he knew this illegal mining and slavery was but a small part of what was . . . what must be . . . going on.

No, he would just have to keep on trying, keep on working. On second thought, he had done pretty well so far, at that—he felt he had a right to feel good about that.

But he wasn't done yet, by a whole tankful of fuel.

The problem stayed with him even in sleep, but in the morning he had an idea.

As soon as he got his crew down into the mine and working, he got out the frequency-transformer, and called Geck to him.

"Can you find out what is happening on other parts of Guddu?"

The native's answers stunned him.

"Yes, An-yon, all we can mind-talk with any Guddu anywhere. What you wish to know?"

# Chapter 16

The knowledge that these Guddus of Algon were telepathic rocked George Hanlon back on his heels. That was a thing he had never even imagined. They were such a simple, almost childlike race, that such an ability was farthest from his thoughts.

"If you can talk with your minds?" he asked Geck in wonder, "why do you bother to speak with the voice to each other?"

"Because mind-talk more tiring to we," came the simple explanation. "It take much of we's forces. Us grow weak after much of them."

"That makes me hesitate to ask you to do any of it, then," the young SS man said. "I was hoping you could find out for me how many mines are operated on the planet, and if all of them are using you Guddus as slaves."

"Oh, yes, An-yon, me know that already," Geck's peculiar little face, which had become so friendly to Hanlon through long association, broke out into a smile that was quickly shadowed by sorrow at thought of the plight of his people. "There is nine mines. Human masters make Guddu work in all of they."

"Nine, eh?" Hanlon thought swiftly for a moment. "Do they all produce the same ores as this one?"

"Will have to find that for you, An-yon. You wait short space of time."

The Greenie grew silent and strained with concentration. Hanlon probed into the native's mind, wondering if he could follow it. And haltingly at first, but with growing ability as he learned the pattern, he found he could ride along on that telepathic beam.

The thoughts were far too swift for him to catch more

117

than an occasional concept, but he was thrilled to realize he was actually telepathing, even though at second-hand.

One after another mind he could feel joining in that conference. There was much hostility and great fear when Geck first tried to explain about the human who was their friend, and had learned to talk with them. The Guddus on the other end of that "line" were tremendously skeptical, afraid, and very, very suspicious of the motives of any human being.

But Geck was eloquent and persuasive. Before long their fears began to lessen, and later they seemed to accept his assurance that "An-yon" was, indeed, both friendly and anxious to help them escape their slavery.

"The human An-yon is but one of the most of humans who are kind and just and ethical," he was surprised to hear Geck telepathing when he got so he could understand. "It is the few, such as those others who are here, who are not. These are bad men who come here just to get things for own selfish ends, and the good men, who are most, will stop them as soon as they can. An-yon come here just for that, to find out what those bad men do, and to stop them."

That speech was another shock to Hanlon—he had never told Geck all that.

The distant natives finally bowed to Geck's importunings, and gave him the specific information for which he was asking because the friendly human wanted to know it.

There were two other mines that produced the same uraninite ore as the one at which Hanlon was stationed. There were three iron mines, and Hanlon was not too surprised to learn that at each of these mines smelters had been erected. He learned that humans were used mostly in the mills, the natives being used only for outside labor because they could not stand the heat.

"We burn quickly," was the sad, horrified thought.

There were three other mines, but the natives did not know the English or Greek names for the metals found there. Even after considerable questioning by the roundabout "Hanlon to Geck to the Guddus back to Geck back to Hanlon" method, he still couldn't get that specific information.

"If it isn't tiring you too much, Geck, please ask them

if there is any building going on besides the smelters at the iron mines?" Hanlon requested.

Soon other minds about the planet were coming in, and the story began to unfold—there were several factories making many machines. But none of the natives had the least idea what kind, or for what purpose they were being made.

"Think they are going to be put in great metal huts humans are making," one thought ran, and Hanlon quickly grabbed onto that.

"What sort of metal huts?"

"Things that look like huge eggs."

"Space ships, you mean?"

Another thought broke in. "Yes, they like ships human come in, but much greater."

Hanlon fumed. Oh, if only he could see . . . but wait, maybe he could get the information he needed. "Ask if anyone is looking at one of those 'eggs' right now," he commanded Geck through the transformer.

"Yes, An-yon, many Guddu right at edge of great place of making. Brother of me, Nock, him there."

"Ask him, please, to describe what he sees. Maybe that will give me a good picture of what it is."

"Will be glad to try, but not knowing your language and having no compare your measurement to ours, am not sure can do what you wish," he felt Nock say.

This, too, surprised Hanlon. That native certainly had a real mind, to grasp that difficulty so well, and to realize the limitations of telepathic communications with one alien to his race.

"Please picture it in your mind as you see it, and use some common objects of the planet for comparison of their sizes," Hanlon urged through Geck's mind. "That way I think we can get along."

Almost instantly a picture of a gigantic egg formed in his mind, but with enough variations from an actual egg so that Hanlon realized it was, indeed, a space ship the native was viewing. Soon Hanlon saw a great tree pictured beside the ship, and at the base of the tree a native was standing.

Quickly Hanlon estimated. The adult natives he had seen were almost all about six feet tall. As nearly as he could judge that tree was a good fifteen times the height of the Guddu, and the ship was the same height as the tree, and nearly three times as long.

Wow! What a ship! But it must be wrong. Even the largest Corps' warships were nowhere near that huge. Nor were even any of the biggest freighters he had ever seen. He must be getting his measurements wrong.

He called Geck, using the transformer. "Are you seeing what I am in Nock's mind?"

"Yes, An-yon, and you is figure right. Is that big."

Hanlon slowly shook his head in amazement. If that was meant for a warship, it certainly spelled trouble for someone. He thought seriously for several moments, then telepathed Nock. "Is there more than one ship being built?"

"Oh, yes, there are many many." The picture built up of a whole row of ships, and Hanlon counted swiftly.

*Eighteen!*

For what purpose was such a fleet being built? Men would not defy the I-S C and the Federated Planets this way merely for business reasons, he felt sure. There certainly was a plot being hatched—and what a plot!

He felt Geck's hand on his arm, and heard his voice. "Are two more places where humans build many ship, An-yon. While you think me talk many minds. One place are fourteen more great ones. At other are many many many small ones five to ten Guddu long."

Shock on shock! Someone was builing a tremendous fleet here! He *must* get that news to Corps headquarters as quickly as possible. If those ships were once finished, they would be able to dominate the system. For the Corps had only a nominal fleet. They had never needed a large one.

To the best of his knowledge the Corps had only thirty-one first-line battleships, much smaller than these. The Fleet also had fifty heavy cruisers, a hundred and fifty light cruisers, and a thousand scouts running from one-man up to twelve-man size.

"Please find out if any of those ships they are building have ever left the ground."

"Some little ones only," Geck reported after awhile.

"Some few disappear into sky then come back after time, then do same again."

Trial trips, or training trips for the crews, Hanlon deduced.

Well, he had some data now, at least. Enough so that once he got that news to Headquarters they would attack this place in force great enough to stop this work . . . IF . . . he could get word to them soon enough.

"Let's see now," he figured quickly. "I've been here almost twelve weeks. That means another six or seven until I'm supposed to be eligible to get back to Simonides. Hmmm. Wish I knew how near finished those big battle-wagons are."

More moments of intense thought. "I don't dare take the chance of trying to sneak off to the yards," he reasoned logically. "I've got to do everything I can to make sure I get my trip back when my eighteen weeks are up. If I got caught off bounds that would ruin everything—I'd really be in a mess."

Also, even if he could get to the shipyards, the moment he was spotted trying to get inside any of those ships he would undoubtedly be killed by guards who would certainly shoot first and ask questions later—if any.

Nor were there any longer any native birds or animals left on Algon he could use—he had learned that the men had killed them off soon after they arrived.

"No, I'll just have to keep on trying, and get what dope I can without exposing myself. With a month and a half I should be able to get a lot more, and with what I already know, the Corps top brass will take steps, but fast!"

Suddenly a new idea sprang into his mind. Where was "here?" In his excitement and planning he had entirely forgotten to finish figuring out that point.

That evening after dinner he stayed outside, ostensibly walking about aimlessly, in reality looking at and studying the stars when he was sure no one was watching him.

He couldn't spot any of the more familiar constellations such as the Big Dipper, Bear, or the Southern Cross. He knew he was far to one side of the galaxy from Terra—that while from there one could see the "front" of those configurations, now he would be getting a "sidewise" view. But he could identify quite a few of the bigger suns and distant nebulae.

He picked out several blue-white and red giants he was sure he knew. That was Andromeda off there; that one was undoubtedly Orion—no other contained so many 4.0 to 5.2 stars, beside the gigantic Rigel, Betelgeuse and Bellatrix.

Good, he could fix all that in his mind well enough to draw it when he got back, and the Corps planeto-graphers certainly would pin-point this system from those directions. Distance—let's see? He strained to remember the time it had taken that freighter to come here, and estimated that, with its slower speed, this world was somewhere between ten and fifteen lights. He would time it more carefully, going back, and estimate the ship's speed as closely as possible.

Young George Hanlon was maturing swiftly under the stress of the tremendous task he was attemping. He was learning that he must think and plan well ahead of time. He realized he could not afford to make any serious mistakes, lest not only his task remain uncompleted, but his life be forfeit as well.

He knew now that it was absolutely imperative that he get back to Simonides at the earliest possible moment, and that the way to be sure of this was to so impress Philander that he would feel duty-bound to give Hanlon his vacation at end of the minimum time.

So Hanlon devoted many hours of serious thought to this problem, and finally figured out several courses of action. The next day, as soon as his shift was over, Hanlon walked across the compound and knocked on the door of the headquarters office. When bade to enter he did so, hat in hand.

"Have you got a half hour or so to talk, Mr. Philander, sir?" he asked. "I've got a couple of ideas I'd like to gab with you about, that I think might speed up production even more."

The man looked up in surprise, and his eyes bored deeply, suspiciously into Hanlon's. "You think you can tell me how to run my job?" he rasped.

"Oh, no, sir. I didn't mean about the engineering or

supervision. It's about handling the natives, and getting more out of them. You've said I was getting out more ore than the others, and I think perhaps I've got a few ideas —a sort of hunch about making the Greenies themselves more productive."

"Well, come in, come in then. What is it?"

"I've been doing a lot of thinking about the Greenies, sir. You remember I thought they were vegetable matter, and the way they feed themselves they'd need ground that either has lots of natural chemicals in it, or that has been well-fertilized, to keep 'em well and strong. That being the case, the dirt that forms the floors of their huts and stockades would very quickly become exhausted of those vital chemicals, and the natives would begin suffering from malnutrition, it seems to me. My gang has been slowing down recently, although they still seem to be trying as hard as ever."

"Why . . . why, yes," the superintendent's eyes had widened in surprise as Hanlon talked. "That makes sense. Imagine none of us thinking of that! But then, we've always thought of them merely as dumb beasts."

"So I've been wondering if it wouldn't be a good idea either to move the stockades every month or so, or else let the natives 'feed' out in the open jungle every day—the sunlight would probably help them, too, being vegetable. They could be tied together and guarded, of course, so they couldn't escape."

Philander slumped down into his chair in deep thought, and Hanlon glowed inwardly with the hope that something would come of this plan. It would help him with Philander, if it worked. Also, it would help the Guddus, for Geck had often grown almost hysterical when complaining about the terrible hunger they all felt so continuously.

Suddenly Philander sat erect. "I believe we've got a few sacks of commercial nitrates in the storehouse. Let's experiment and see if they can use that."

He rose purposefully from his desk and the two hurried to one of the warehouses. There Philander soon found the sacks of chemical, and Hanlon carried one as they went to the corral.

"May we try it on my crew first, sir?" he asked anxiously. "They seem to sort of like me, and I've learned more or less how to guess their reactions by their facial movements, so I think I could tell whether they like it or not."

"Sure, that's a good idea," and they went on to the compound that housed Hanlon's special crew.

Inside, while Hanlon apparently chose at random, it was actually Geck to whom he beckoned. When the native approached, feigning fear and reluctance—Hanlon hid a sudden grin at Geck's unexpected acting brilliance—the young man opened the sack and poured out a little of the nitrate.

He stooped over and stuck his fingers into the stuff then rose and gestured to Geck to put his feeding fingers into it the same way. Meanwhile Hanlon was telepathing the exact information to his friend, as best he could with his limited ability.

Gingerly Geck stooped, and after a few false starts finally put one of his fingers into the little pile of nitrate, and activated the feeding sensories. For a few moments he stood thus, doubtfully, then his manner clearly indicated joy and surprised happiness. He began working that little triangular-shaped mouth, and the others crowded closer.

Telepathically he informed Hanlon that this was wonderful—exactly the food element the natives needed so desperately.

"It seems to think it's all okay," Hanlon said aloud to Philander. "I'll spread out a little more for them all," and without waiting for permission he made a long, narrow pile of the fertilizer clear across the width of the hut. Instantly the rest of the natives crowded along that line and stuck their feeding fingers into it. Soon their silly-looking faces expressed their equivalent of blissful smiles of complete satisfaction, and Hanlon's mind was suffused with thoughts of pleasure and gratitude for his kindness.

# Chapter 17

**S**UPERINTENDENT PHILANDER STOOD WATCHING the natives feeding, and he could not help seeing how they appeared to appreciate the new food. After some time he said admiringly, "It looks like you've hit on something, George. If it continues to work out, we'll feed all of 'em this stuff, and I'll requisition plenty more next time the freighter comes in."

They left the compound, carefully locking both gates behind them, and walked back to the office. Once there, Hanlon said, "I see you have a chess set, sir. Do you play? I love the game."

"You do?" Philander's eyes gleamed. "It's been a long time since there was anyone here who did."

"Then I hope you'll let me come in occasionally for a game. I get lonesome here. The other guards aren't worth talking to, and I'm not educated enough in science or technology to get in on the arguments of the engineers and other technies."

"Sure, sure, come in any time. I'll be mighty glad to have you, for I love chess. I get lonesome, too, and I have to stay a whole year at a time. Feel free to come in any evening."

Back in his room Hanlon left tremendously satisfied with the evening's work. He had done something for the natives that would help make their intolerable situation more bearable until the time came when they could be freed of their slavery . . . and he had made a new friend who could prove very useful.

He was very anxious for the next work-period to come, so he could talk to Geck via the voice-transformer. For he was not yet adept enough at telepathy to be sure he had

125

got all the information needed about the use of nitrates in the Guddu's diet.

But the next day when he went to herd his crew from their compound and down into the mine, he could not help noticing at first glance how much sprightlier they looked than the other crews. The minute they had reached the stope he unearthed the machine from its hiding place and got into conversation with the friendly Guddu.

"The food stuff?" he asked eagerly. "Is it something you can use?"

"Oh, yes. An-yon," Geck almost sputtered in his eagerness, and words tumbled out so swiftly Hanlon could hardly translate them. "It are wonderful! Can you fix so all we can have?"

"Yes, they'll all be fed rations of it from now on, although perhaps not much until the ship can bring more from another planet. I don't know how much we have on hand. But the Boss-man liked my idea, and is going to see to it that there is always some on hand for all the natives. He'll probably spread the word to the other mines and factories, too."

"Almost us ingest too many last dark," Geck gave what Hanlon knew was a shamefaced laugh. "It such very good eat us become . . ." he hesitated.

"Drunk, you mean?" Hanlon laughed. "I can see it might do that to you. You'll have to warn the others about that."

They chatted away for some minutes, about how much the Guddus appreciated Hanlon's thoughtfulness.

"Say, I just wondered," Hanlon interrupted Geck's thanks. "Do you have any idea where your planet is located in space? I mean, do you know the suns closest to yours, anything about their distances or magnitudes?"

Geck's thoughts and expression were a blank, and it took most of the work-period even to make him understand what Hanlon was trying to ask. When he did finally manage to grasp the thought-concept, his answer was a decided negative.

"No, An-yon, us know nothing about other sun other planet. Before humans come suppose we only intelligent life anywhere. Things you call suns us thought little fires light sky at night. Wonder many night who build. Wonder what is burn where is nothing. Wonder why only one big fire come day. Wonder why big fire die come night."

Hanlon's disappointment about that was tempered somewhat when the checker came running into his room where he was resting before dinner, to tell him that his crew had suddenly got out almost half a ton more ore that day than any previous record he had made.

A new cook had come to the mine recently. He had a fox terrier, and Hanlon got into the habit of playing with the dog, to keep up his ability to handle animal minds, and to learn more of the technique. He was always careful to say out loud the command for whatever trick he wanted the animal to perform, but actually he was controlling its brain and nerves and muscles.

One evening he was working thus with the dog when Gorton, his head-wound still bandaged, came into the messhall. Seeing Hanlon with the terrier, his heavy lip curled.

"So th' fair-haired boy's also a animal trainer, eh?"

"That he is," Cookie said from the doorway leading into the kitchen. "And good, too! He's got Brutus doing things I never knew a dog could do."

Gorton sneered again. "Teachin' tricks t' a dog is kid stuff."

"Can you do it?" the cook asked sarcastically.

"Who'd bother t' try?"

Hanlon looked up, blandly. "You couldn't expect that of Mr. Gorton, Cookie. To teach an animal to do tricks you have to know more than it does."

"Why, you . . ." Gorton started forward, his face aflame, while the other men roared with laughter at the rough wit.

But the big guard did not reach Hanlon. One of the newer guards, a giant Swede named Jenssen, stopped him. "Aw, lay off the kid, Gort. He's okay. That stunt of feeding the Greenies fertilizer makes 'em turn out lots more work, and we'll get us bigger bonuses 'cause of it."

But Gorton was not the type to know when to quit. Nor was he high enough in the ethical scale to know appreciation for the fact that it was the very man he had been reviling who was the first to go to his aid when he was hurt.

Hanlon had come to realize that the big man was determined to provoke him to another fight. He knew that tempers were edgy and explosive in this enervating heat, and usually tried to bear Gorton's insults and petty meannesses in silence. He wouldn't demean himself by descending to the big guard's low level . . . although occasionally, when the heat was too much even for him, as tonight, he couldn't resist making some answer.

Gorton, he had long since decided, was one of those men who, having nothing of worth to offer the world, did their utmost to tear down and humiliate anyone who had. And his smallness of soul and intellect were shown by the sort of tricks he was continually pulling, thinking them smart.

Such as scrawling with chalk on Hanlon's room door, "Super's pet"; continually upsetting Hanlon's beverage cup, or "accidentally" dropping things in Hanlon's plate of food.

The young SS man could have moved to another place at the table, but he wouldn't give the big guard that satisfaction.

But one of Gordon's tricks backfired to such an extent that it had disastrous results for Gorton himself. That was the night he, knowing that Hanlon had been the last at the compound, sneaked out and unlocked all the gates. He figured, of course, that it would be apparent to everyone that it was Hanlon's rank carelessness that had allowed all the Greenies to escape.

But to the surprise of everyone—except Hanlon—not a single one had left; all were inside their huts the next morning.

Philander came running when he heard about it. "Who did it?" he demanded angrily.

"Th' punk there, o' course!" Gorton sneered.

Philander swivelled about, surprise on his face. "You, George? Did you forget to lock the gates?"

"No, sir, I locked them all when I went in to dinner."

"He's lyin'. He was th' last one t' bring up his gang."

"That's true, I was. But I know I locked all the gates very carefully, as always."

One of the engineers spoke up. "I saw him doing it, Pete. I also saw one of the other guards leave the messhall for a few minutes just before we sat down to eat. When he came back I saw him grinning mysteriously as though very self-satisfied about something."

"Who was that?"

"Sorry, I name no names."

"I tell," big Jenssen spoke up. "It was Gort. He's got it in for George. He's one big fool!"

Philander wheeled in rage. "I told you, you brainless slob, to leave Hanlon alone, and by Jupiter, I mean it! Cut it out! One more stunt, and you go into irons, then back to Sime for an interview with His Highness. You go back next trip anyway. I'm done with you."

The rest of the men stood by in hostile silence, and it was clear from their attitudes that this time Gorton had gone too far. How it happened none of the natives had run away, puzzled them all.

But Hanlon guessed, and when he had taken his crew down to work he called Geck to him, and by means of the transformer asked about it.

"Was one Guddu in hut by main gate who first see gate were open. Him mind-tell all we to run far into forest. This crew us stop all they. Tell other Guddu how kind are you. How you get we 'oigm'-food. Tell how you's work to make all we free; make free all Guddu everywhere. Us say maybe so we's all get free now small time. But say come humans with shock-rod, hunt we, hurt we, make we work more hard, be more cruel to we. Say then plan of you never get chance to make all we free all time."

Hanlon bowed his head in silent thanks for the tremendous compliment. "I only hope I can justify your faith in me, Geck," he said humbly. "It will be a miracle if I can bring it about, but I certainly intend to keep on trying. It will take some time, you know that. I can't possibly do anything until after I leave here. But if it's humanly possible, I'll bring the fleet here to free you."

"Us know will be hard, that maybeso it never come we be free," the Guddu said. "But us know you are only hope. So us help you all us can. Guddu in mines try get more rock out as you say. But Guddu who help humans build big egg you call 'ships' do most. Each day some of they find way break something, do wrong thing. Two Guddu spoil much metal when jump in vat where metal be melt."

"Oh, no!" Hanlon cried in shocked anguish. "That was wonderfully brave of them, but none of the others must ever do things like that! Tell them not to sacrifice their lives that way! I feel sure from all the reports it isn't needed. I'll be going back in another few weeks, and the humans won't have any of those biggest ships ready by then. Those are the only ones we need to fear—the little ships don't count."

It was too bad Hanlon did not know what else the humans were building, besides ships, at the shipyards.

Hanlon's campaign to "get in good" with Philander was bearing tasty fruit, for the two were becoming fast friends. They spent many evenings over a hotly-contested chess board. It was plain now that the nervous, worried superintendent felt he could relax in the company of this young, naive guard, for the latter was so patently no challenge to his position. Besides, it was also very evident that he *liked* Hanlon as a man. Day by day his attitude grew more fatherly.

Hanlon, on his part, came to realize more the true, innate measure of Philander's inherent worth as a man, a gentleman, and an engineer. He had a fine mind, was well read, and thought deeply on many subjects outside his own technical line.

"All he needs are some psychiatric treatments to reduce that awful inferiority complex of his," Hanlon mused one night as he walked back slowly to his room. "Then he'll really be the big, fine man he's capable of being, and will forget all this conspiracy nonsense."

Thus Hanlon felt he was taking no special chance one night when the two were standing on the little porch of the office, their game ended, and Hanlon about to leave. He glanced up at the brilliant night sky.

"Sure looks different here than it does back on Terra," he said conversationally. "Naturally it would, seeing we're so far away from there. But I never get tired of looking at it, and trying to see if I can figure out some of the brighter suns." He pointed to one bright star directly overhead. "That's Sirius, I know. It's always directly above you."

Philander laughed heartily. "No, Sirius is almost exactly opposite. Don't forget we're about a hundred light years out from Sol."

Hanlon made himself look crestfallen. "And there I was sure I knew one of 'em, at least." He yawned pretentiously. "Well, guess I'll hit the hay. Reckon the stars'll stay put, whether I can pick 'em out or not."

Philander laughed again, and clapped him on the back in comradely fashion. "I wouldn't wonder. Goodnight, George."

"'Night, Mr. Philander." And as Hanlon walked back to his own room his heart was light. He'd learned another important fact about their location in space—the approximate distance from Sol.

# Chapter 18

A FEW NIGHTS LATER ONE OF THE JUNIOR ENGI-neers came running into the office where Hanlon and Philander were playing chess.

"Trouble down in Stope Four," he gasped.

Philander jumped up, upsetting the board. He grabbed his glo-light and started out.

"Want me along, sir?" Hanlon asked.

"Might as well," and Hanlon ran with them.

Down in the mine they found, after examination, that it was not as bad as it at first seemed. Some timbers had rotted away—or had not been good wood in the first place —and a rock fall had occurred. But once they started working at it, they found it not too big. Hanlon was sent running for the rest of the men, and in a few hours everything was all tight again.

Back in the office Hanlon picked up the fallen chess pieces while Philander and the engineers talked for some time. When they left Hanlon asked, "Want to finish the game—or rather, since the board was upset, want to play another?"

"Better make it a rain-check. I've got some paper work I should do. Make it tomorrow."

"That's okay with me. I'll go hit the hay."

"Thanks for your help tonight, George. You pitched in so gladly, while the others were surly and grumbling. It was very noticeable, and I appreciate it. You're a good kid. Wish I had one just like you."

Hanlon flushed a bit, and couldn't meet his friend eye to eye. "I was glad to do it," he said lamely. " 'Night," and he ran out. Blast it, he thought, I hate using Pete that way, 'cause he's really a swell egg underneath. But the job's more important.

A few nights later they had finished the second game, and the elder had won both. He was consequently in very good humor, for the two were so evenly matched it was seldom either ever won two games in the same evening.

Philander leaned back in his chair and smiled at the younger man. "Well, George, the freighter'll be here in three days, and I'm sending you back for your vacation."

"Gee, thanks, Chief. That's swell of you. I'm going to miss you, but I'll admit I'll be glad to get away from this awful climate for a while. This place sure gets my goat—I can't seem to get used to it all."

"Then you won't want to come back?" There was disappointment in the question.

"Oh, no, I didn't mean that. I sure will be back if I can make it. Maybe this job isn't exactly what I'd dreamed about," he had to hedge that statement a bit, and tried to make a sincere-sounding explanation, "but that thousand credits a month is!"

"That reminds me—I want to be sure to recommend you for a good bonus. You deserve it more'n any guard we've ever had here. Then, too, your ideas of rotating your crew, and especially that fertilizer deal, have raised the effective work-life and speed of the natives almost thirty percent. I figured it out, and they'll be getting off cheap if they give you what I'm recommending—two months pay as a bonus."

"Yowie!" Hanlon yelled, making his face show excitement, and that curious avarice he had so carefully built up in these suspicious men's minds. "That'll make me six thou in four months. I'll be rich yet!"

"You and your urge for money," Philander laughed, yet there was a curious undertone of almost-contempt in his voice. "Why're you so hipped on that subject?"

Hanlon grinned and misquoted, "Life is real, life is earnest, and the gravy is my goal." Then he sobered and said, "'Cause with money you can do anything. When I've made a big pile, then I can go where I want to go, be what I want to be, and make people know I'm somebody."

Philander shrugged. "Maybe you're right, but I'd say there were better ways, George."

Hanlon looked doubtful. "I have the utmost respect for your ideas and greater experience, sir, but what's better than a big wad of credits."

Philander looked more seriously thoughtful than Hanlon had ever seen him before. He was silent a moment, then answered slowly, "This may sound 'old-mannish,' but I believe steady advancement in whatever work you choose; growing knowledge of many things; creative imagination put to constructive use; the growing respect and consequent advance in responsibility from your employers if you're working for someone, or from your neighbors if you're in business for yourself—those things are, in my opinion, of much greater value than the mere accumulation of money. And the best part of it is, that if you grow in those ways, that extra money will come to you, but merely as a corollary addition to the greater achievements."

"I see your point," Hanlon was greatly impressed by Philander's earnestness. "Maybe you're right. I'm still just a kid, I guess, with a kid's immature outlook. That's why I appreciate your friendship and advice so much, sir. You've been almost like a second father to me." This was honest—he liked Philander now more than ever.

The look on the elder's face, too, defied description, but that he was secretly pleased was evident.

"Well, run along then, and I'll get at that letter. Meanwhile get your things packed, so you'll be ready to leave when the ship comes. And George, my boy, I do hope you come back. It'll be mighty lonely here without you."

"I'll certainly do my best to get back, sir. Goodnight, and thanks again . . . for everything."

Hanlon hated that seeming lie, and as he walked slowly back to his room he determined to get the man away from those plotters, and into a better and more legitimate position.

He would certainly so recommend to the Secret Service High Command after this mess was cleaned up.

The next days Hanlon spent almost his entire shift-time underground talking earnestly to Geck.

"I want to impress on the minds of you and all the natives here that I'll be working my hardest for them every minute I'm gone," he said impressively. "Don't let them do anything foolish unless or until it becomes completely sure that I've failed. If I can do anything at all, it should be within a quarter year after I leave, and probably much sooner. If I succeed, you'll all be free, and these men either chased off your planet or killed."

"All we understand, An-yon. We know you are true friend, know you want to help us. We will keep working, make no attempts to escape. We know if do we just be killed, or hunted and caught again. Condition of we before you come so bad we had come to feel only end for us be death of race. Now you bring hope. Now we know most humans good people, so we wait in hope you soon succeed."

"That's the spirit. I know it's tough on all of you, but I also know what the Inter-Stellar Corps is, and what they can and will do when they learn of your plight."

He linked his mind with Geck's as the latter telepathed the natives in other parts of the planet, and was thus enabled to get final descriptions of what they could tell of what was being done at each mine and factory and shipyard. He knew exactly how many ships had been built or were under construction, and approximately how far along the hulls of the big ones were completed. He was also able to get a very good general knowledge of the size and structural description of each type of vessel.

But of their armaments or propulsive methods he had not been able to get any information—such things were too far beyond the natives' simple abilities to describe or picture for him.

Hanlon's ability to telepath, through Geck, was growing much stronger, although he was still not able to telepath direct to any of the distant Guddus. He could, however, do so to some extent to one close by.

But he still could not read anything in a human mind except the surface thoughts. And how he could use that ability! With that, his task would be much simpler.

But he had learned to be content with what he had, realizing it was undoubtedly unique in human history. It had brought him this far along, and he had collected a lot of information which he could not have gained in any other manner—information that he could report to the Corps as soon as he got back to Simonides and had the chance to go to the bank or contact them in some other way.

"Liberation Day," as Hanlon had taken to calling it in his mind, finally arrived. He was all packed and waiting for the ship. When it was sighted he and Philander went to the field to meet it.

When the captain came out, the three stood in conversation while the crew hurriedly unloaded the supplies they had brought, and those leaving had gone aboard. The captain handed Philander some letters, but the latter shoved them in his pocket for the time being, without stopping to look at them.

Finally it was time for blast-off, and Hanlon said his last farewells to the superintendent, then went in to stow his bags in his stateroom and prepare for take-off. He had expected to be locked in again, and merely tried the door out of curiosity. But to his surprise it wasn't locked, so he went out. He was wise enough not to attempt to invade the control room, but did hunt up a viewing-screen and strap himself into the chair before it.

He manipulated the dials and had just got an outside view as the pilot began activating the tubes. Hanlon saw Philander come running from the little path through the jungle, back toward the field, waving a letter, trying to attract attention.

But evidently neither the captain, pilot nor any watch officer saw him, for at that moment the great wash of flame from the tubes blotted out the scene, and Hanlon was forced deeply into his acceleration chair as the ship lifted gravs.

The trip back was uneventful. Hanlon kept careful track of the time, and strained all his spaceman's senses properly to evaluate their speed. As the ship braked for the landing on Simonides he completed his calculations, and was quite sure the distance between the two planets was twelve and a quarter light years, plus or minus not over two percent, and that Algon was somewhere near right ascension eighteen hours, and declination plus fifteen degrees.

As he passed through the airlock and started down the plank, he was surprised and a bit dismayed to see Panek and two of the other gunmen he had seen in that back room, waiting for him, their faces impassive and un-readable.

"A welcoming committee, eh?" he greeted them with a smile that tried to cover his disappointment. "Hiya, Panek! Hi, fellows!"

But his heart was doing flip-flops. These men were not here just because they were glad to see him, of that he was sure. He probed their minds and even before Panek spoke, he knew.

"The boss sent us to bring you to see him first thing, the boss did," Panek's voice was gruff, yet somewhat friendly.

"That's mighty nice of him," Hanlon tried not to let his feelings show, but to take this as a natural courtesy. But he had so much wanted to get to the bank imme-diately. "I was coming to report, of course," he com-mented. "Got a letter for him from Superintendent Philander. Besides, I got a flock of credits coming. Boy, did I earn 'em! That's a stinking, hot planet up there. It'll be good seeing the bright lights again, besides living in a decent climate once more."

The two men grunted a mysterious laugh, but Panek merely indicated the way to the aircar. Again Hanlon was blindfolded, but now he didn't care—he knew the location of this crater field.

There was silence during most of the trip. Hanlon bab-bled away at first, but when no one answered him he grad-ually slowed his words and finally shut up entirely.

His mind probings told him he was in for a rough time, and he got the feeling he was not supposed to be there at all, for some reason.

"Oh, oh!" he thought, almost in panic. "Something's wrong. Did I slip somewhere? Have they got wind of what I've learned? But how . . . how could they?"

Instead of taking him to the back room of the Bacchus, Hanlon found when the blindfold was finally removed that he was in a stone-walled room that he sensed was a sort of cellar in some huge building. It was bare of furniture except for two chairs and the glo-lights, one of which was on a standard like a spotlight.

Before he had time to try to puzzle things out, the door opened and the man he had thought of merely as "the leader" came in and sat down in one of the chairs. He gestured, and the men pushed Hanlon into the facing seat, and adjusted the glo-light so it shone in his eyes. Then ranged themselves behind him.

"So, you got back?" the Leader said softly.

"Sure," Hanlon made himself act as though nothing was out of the way, but it was an effort to smile and talk naturally when his mouth was suddenly dry and his nerves tightened almost to the screaming point. "My time was up, so Mr. Philander sent me back. I've got a letter for you from him."

He started to reach into his pocket, but Panek slapped his hand down, and snaked the letter out, handing it to the Leader, who opened it and read it silently.

Then the man looked up, his face puzzled. "You seem to have . . . uh . . . done very well there," he said almost pleasantly. "Our superintendent reports you made an excellent guard. He seems very pleased with you."

"I told you I'd do everything I could to make good," Hanlon answered, but now he made his voice sound very aggrieved. "What's the big idea of all this? Seems like a mighty funny reception, after I tried so hard. Why that light in my eyes, and those thugs ready to slug me if I bat an eye-lash. It's almost like you don't trust me, or something?"

"I'm still not altogether sure we do," the Leader said slowly.

"Still harping on that?" Hanlon demanded hotly.

"What makes you think I'm not on the up and up? I worked hard on that stinking hot planet. I got out more ore'n anyone else ever did. And my suggestion about nitrates . . ."

"Ah, yes, the matter of the . . . uh . . . fertilizer. What made you bring that up?"

"The minute I saw those Greenies I guessed they were animated trees. When I saw how they fed themselves by sticking their fingers in the hut floor, I figured the dirt would gradually lose whatever nourishment it contained, same as a farmer's fields soon lose their fertility. All plants I know about extract nitrogen and other minerals from the soil. So I figured the Greenies would need fertilizer to make up for the depleted soil in their huts. It seemed simple to me."

"Ummm. You were right, apparently. It was a great contribution to our work, and we are grateful." He looked at Hanlon a long moment, then asked sharply, "How did Rellos die?"

"A dog tore out his throat."

"We know that—but you said you killed him."

"Who d'you suppose sicced the dog on him? We were walking down the street, and I kicked the dog's pup to death. When she charged, I pushed Rellos in her path, and it was him the dog killed."

"Ah! Good! Very unusual! Most . . . uh . . . ingenious!" The Leader seemed pleased, but slowly his smile died and he frowned again. "All this makes me want to believe you, Hanlon, but somehow I can't seem to rid myself of the belief that you still are connected with the Corps. Oh, I know," as Hanlon started to protest, "all about your dismissal and disgrace, and the fight you had with some of your former classmates a few days later. Incidentally, wasn't it rather straining coincidence that it was an admiral who came along just in time to save you? You see, all that could easily have been done on purpose. I'm . . . uh . . . not that simple, young man."

"No, but you're nuts, figuring that way!" disgustedly.

"I think you will find out differently," the tone sent shivers through the young SS man's nerves, and he had difficulty controlling the impulse to wet his suddenly dry lips "I may be wrong—I hope most sincerely that I am—

but I haven't so far been able to bring myself to feel so. But I intend to know for sure before we leave this room. Panek, bring in our other . . . uh . . . guest."

Hanlon heard the gunman leave, and in a moment return. He appeared in Hanlon's line of vision, pushing before him a manacled man.

At sight of that other man, Hanlon had to gasp.

# Chapter 19

"OH!" THE LEADER SAID TRIUMPHANTLY AS he saw George Hanlon's start of surprise. "I see you recognize our guest."

"Sure I know him," Hanlon snapped, rigidly forcing himself into control. "That's Abrams. I thought I killed him."

"Ah, now, did you so?" Again the Leader smiled, but this time grimly. "Now we come to the meat of the matter. "You say you thought you killed him, but you know you didn't. Your pretended assassination in such a clever manner was all a ruse—you didn't poison him at all. You merely pretended to put something in his cup."

"That's a lie. Maybe it didn't work on him, but I did . . ."

"Sorry, Mr. Hanlon," the trembling Abrams whined the interruption. "I was forced to tell the whole story to His Highness after he found out where I was hiding."

*His Highness!*

So this was the fabulous monster of whom everyone was so afraid. Hanlon's heart sank to his knees. What chance did he have now? He would never get out of this alive, nor get his report to the Corps.

"Yes, Mr. Hanlon," that silky voice mimicked meaningly, and venomously. "We have . . . uh . . . ways of making people talk. This Abrams, like a fool, was not content to continue working as my secretary. He had to get foolish notions of ethics and patriotism, and try to . . . uh . . . object to some of my policies. Why did you let him think you were still a Corpsman . . . if you're not?" he snapped suddenly.

Hanlon made himself stare back insolently. Maybe they would kill him . . . no, be honest, undoubtedly they would . . . but by the Shade of Snyder they weren't going to make him show the fear he felt.

"Use your head, Pal. I had to make an impression on Panek so he'd introduce me to someone here on Sime who'd show me how to make some fast, big money, which is all I'm after," he retorted with a bravado he certainly didn't feel, but which he hoped would make them think he did. "When I found Panek was going to bump off Abrams, I horned in on it. And what easier way to make Abrams play ball with me—I had nothing against him, and didn't want to really kill him—than to let him think I was still a Corpsman, after he'd seen me when I was still a cadet. I didn't know he'd turn yellow and squeal."

He looked contemptuously at Abrams, then turned back to the leader and made his voice very earnest, very emphatic. "But I've told you the truth! I am not still connected with that rotten outfit, and you're wrong if you think I am!"

"Don't lie to His Highness!" Panek interjected. "He don't like to be lied to, he don't like it."

"Aw shut up and keep out of this, small fry!" Hanlon sneered, and was rewarded with a hard blow on the side of his head that made him wince. But His Highness intervened.

"That will do, Panek. I'll handle this. Now, Hanlon, I think you had better do some very serious thinking. You can see why we are still skeptical of you. Everything points against you . . . uh . . . except your own word, and the fact that you so apparently did work hard and for our best interests at the mine. That point, I readily grant you, is very much in your favor. I am being very patient with you because, if you are telling the truth, you can be a very valuable man to me. You do have real ability, and other assets. But if you are not wholly for us, you are distinctly in our way."

"I tell you . . ."

"Don't interrupt, please. I might inform you that I sent you to the other planet both to test you and to keep you out of the way while we investigated further and I could reach a decision. You were not supposed to come back yet. I sent Philander a letter to that effect, but he space-radioed you were already on the way back when he read it."

A light dawned on Hanlon as memory skipped back to that take-off. Philander had merely stuck the mail in his pocket when it was given him, and evidently started reading it on his way back to the mine. That explained his running back, waving a letter and trying to attract attention just at blast-off.

That small part of his mind that was paying attention to the men in the room heard His Highness say "take Abrams away. He . . . uh . . . is of no further use to us. And wait outside until I call—all of you."

When they had gone His Highness leaned forward, and Hanlon knew he had better pay strict attention and keep his wits about him for any opening to improve his perilous position.

"I'll speak more frankly, now that we are alone, Hanlon. I am impressed with you. I think you have . . . uh . . . tremendous abilities, and I want you on my side. But I have to be sure. I would advise you, for your own good, to be honest and frank with me."

"I am being, but you won't believe me," Hanlon said earnestly. "When I take a man's pay, sir. I give him everything I've got. You gave me a chance at the kind of money I want to make, and I'm doing everything I can to earn both the money and your trust. I was kicked out of the Corps, and I'll do anything I can to get even!"

"As I said before, we have . . . uh . . ways of making you tell us the truth," the Leader continued as though Hanlon had not interrupt, "but you would not be any good either to us or the Corps or yourself if we have to use . . . uh . . . persuasion. I don't want to see you broken. You may remember you once asked me if I could 'dish it out?'. Let me assure you that I can."

"But how can I prove anything when you've already made up your mind not to believe me?" Hanlon asked plaintively. "I'm doing my best to make you believe. I'll admit some of those points you've brought up could look fishy if viewed from one standpoint, but I assure you

you're putting the wrong interpretation on them. If you'll look at them from my viewpoint you'll see they are just as true."

His Highness regarded Hanlon silently but with a steady concentration for some minutes. "That might be true. I had about begun to believe you when we found Abrams, and when we questioned him he . . . uh . . . admitted what you had done, and why. That revived my doubts. Are you willing to be tested under a truth drug?"

Hanlon almost gasped in dismay, but stifled it. He knew only too well the efficacy of modern truth drugs. They would reveal every thought and bit of knowledge he had ever had—all about the Corps, the Secret Service and everything.

That hurt look came back into his face. "You sure are asking a lot, sir," he said. "I haven't anything to conceal from you, but no man likes to have his whole mind invaded that way—all his private thoughts and feelings. I don't see why you need suggest such a thing. I've told you the truth on matters you want to know about."

"You appear to have done so, and I honestly want to believe you. For you see, Hanlon, I want you with me. You're my kind of a man. I like you because you have tremendous drive and imagination and ability—yes, and perhaps a bit because you're the only man I've ever met who wasn't . . . uh . . . afraid of me. I have tremendous plans for the future—and I would like to have you as my chief aide in them. I would train you as you've never guessed it possible for a man to be trained. And then, together, Hanlon, we could rule the Universe!"

But George Hanlon was only half-listening, even to that last, that shocking, that totally unexpected proposition, his real goal. Here was the plot he had been seeking, the plot the Corps needed so desperately to know. Yet his personal crisis was, for the moment, more important if he was ever to be of any further benefit to the Secret Service or the Corps. To use his just-discovered knowledge, something else must come first.

His mind, therefore, was seeking a way out. He well knew that once the truth drug was administered—and this Highness would not now be satisfied with anything less— he was as good as dead. They would find out the truth in minutes, and then would have no other recourse but to kill him.

His spirits sank to nadir with the knowledge that he had failed . . . failed the Secret Service and the Corps, failed his father, failed the Guddus, failed himself. Curiously, perhaps, at that moment the thought of failure was far more important to him than the imminence of death, as such.

He had half-consciously noticed when he first glanced about this room, that there was a small ventilator near the ceiling in one corner. Desperately he pushed his mind through it, and could sense that it opened onto a park-like place, probably around one of the city's palaces.

Hanlon finally heard His Highness call, "Panek, you and the others bring me the hypodermic. We'll have to give him the truth serum. I'm sorry, Hanlon," he addressed himself now to the young man, "but this is the only way. I hope we won't have to use enough to harm you, but that depends on your cooperation. If you will tell us the truth quickly and willingly I can, as I said . . . uh . . . use you, and you will profit greatly by it."

Hanlon didn't struggle when they bound him firmly in the chair with manacles on hands and feet. He knew it would be useless anyway. He let his body slump into his chair, and again directed his mind through that vent. He *must not* let them defeat him! He had to survive—to get word to the Corps!

Then his searching mind contacted another—a weak, primitive one, but a mind. Avidly he fastened onto it, merged with it . . . and found himself inside the brain of one of those Simonidean pigeons.

Ah! This is wonderful! Pigeons seldom fly alone. Where you find one you almost always find a number. Activating the bird's brain he sent out a call to others of its kind that it had found food in abundance. Soon more and more of them flew down to where the now enslaved pigeon was standing, and as each one came, Hanlon sent into its brain all of his mind it would hold.

Inside the cellar room His Highness rose and stepped up to Hanlon's body, the hypodermic in his hand. "Remove his coat and roll up his sleeve," he directed Panek, and the small part of Hanlon's mind still remaining in his body felt the latter doing so, and an instant later, the prick of the needle.

Slowly at first, then with increasing swiftness he felt his remaining mind growing numb and his will weaken. His body slumped against the restraining manacles.

"Can you hear me, George Hanlon?" he dimly heard His Highness' voice.

"Yes." It sounded like a whisper.

"Are you a member of the Inter-Stellar Corps?"

"I . . . I . . .", he struggled not to answer.

"Tell me!"

"I . . . I . . ." and then, in a last desperate effort to keep from telling what he *must not* tell, George Hanlon did a thing he had never dared attempt before. He sent all the remaining parts of his mind into the last of the pigeons.

One of the first birds he had already sent into the ventilator so he could look through it into the room below. He got it there just in time to hear the Leader's gasp of dismay as he saw Hanlon's body slump still further in apparent lifelessness.

"Is he dead, Boss, is he?" he heard Panek's anxious cry.

His Highness felt the pulse in Hanlon's wrist and the one in his throat. "No, he's still alive."

The man stood there in deep thought, his forehead creased with a frown of concentration. "There's something peculiarly wrong here," the Leader finally said aloud. "Something very wrong and very strange. This isn't an ordinary fainting spell. It's . . . uh . . . beyond my previous experience."

He straightened and addressed Hanlon's body once more. "Can you still hear me, George Hanlon?"

There was no answer, no slightest indication that his words were heard. He reached forward and lifted the body into a more upright position in the chair. "Answer me, George Hanlon. Do you hear me? I command you to tell me, are you a Corpsman?"

Still no answer, no twitch of muscle, no movement of awareness. He shook the body a little, and raised his voice still more.

"I demand an answer, George Hanlon! The truth drug must make you speak!"

But only silence, and when he let go of the body it fell backward into the chair, and the head lolled forward as though the neck was broken.

"Let me work on him, Boss," Panek pleaded. "Let me give him a going over, let me."

Barely waiting to see that His Highness did not forbid it, the thug raised a short, ugly piece of rubber hose, and struck the unresisting body again and again—across the face, over the top and back of the head, vicious blows at the ribs and even in the groin.

But he might as well have been pounding a sack of meal. The body sagged beneath the blows, and became bloody and discolored, but no movement—no conscious movement—did it make.

"That will do, Panek," His Highness finally commanded. "That does no good. This I cannot understand, but I do know there is . . . uh . . . something most peculiar here. It is almost as though . . .", he paused and frowned again. "But that is ridiculous!"

"What's ridiculous, Boss, what is?"

"It is almost as though there was . . . uh . . . no mind left in the body," His Highness said slowly. Then, abruptly, "Are you sure that was truth-serum in that hypodermic?"

"You fixed it yourself, Boss."

His Highness wheeled suddenly, rudely awakened from his thinking by the loud *shoo*-ing noise one of the guards was making. He was astonished to see the man making vain motions toward a pigeon whose head was sticking through the ventilator vanes.

But the bird didn't leave.

"Stop it!" the Leader commanded impatiently. "We've more import . . .".

He checked himself, and turned back to stare wonderingly at the bird, which peered back at him with apparently unfrightened, beady eyes, turning its head to first one side and then the other, as though better to see all that was going on.

"That's peculiar," His Highness said thoughtfully. "I never saw a bird act like that before. Hmmm, I wonder? . . . But no, that's absurd."

He turned back to Hanlon's body as though disgusted

with himself for entertaining such a fantastic notion. Hands behind his back, that scowl of concentration engraving deep lines on his face, the Leader paced forth and back across the floor of the little room, his glance ever and again returning to stare in exasperation at that slumped-over, dead-but-alive body.

Who was this amazing young man? What sort of talents and abilities did he possess, that he could react thus to a truth-serum? Had he been so treated by the Corps experts that his mind would be blanked out in such emergencies? Was he some kind of a mutant with powers never before known? Or—startling thought—was he actually a human being at all?

Better than anyone else, His Highness could appreciate the fact that the universe contained many types of sentient and highly mental life other than those originating on Terra. Since he had come here to Simonides, and had wormed his way into the very highest position beneath its emperor—a weak old man he had had no trouble dominating—he was naturally suspicious of anyone who might be attempting to discover and wreck his carefully-laid plans.

Such a one, he was now convinced, was this young Hanlon. It would be the simplest thing to kill this almost-dead body now, but that would not solve this baffling problem. If Hanlon, perhaps others of the Corps had similar powers. No, one with such abilities must not be killed. He must be kept and studied, and the secret learned if possible.

But his thoughts were interrupted by Panek. "That fool bird's still there, still there. Is it another of your pets, Boss?"

His Highness wheeled. He had forgotten the bird. Was it possible that Hanlon had, in some inexplicable manner, transferred . . . on the surface it was an absurd concept. But, there were magicians on his home planet who could do things almost as unfathomable.

He suddenly made up his mind. "Kill it!" he commanded.

Whatever else he was or was not, Panek was fast with a gun. The words were hardly spoken when he had drawn and fired.

# Chapter 20

THE TWENTIETH PART OF HANLON'S MIND activating the pigeon in the ventilator, commanded it to scramble back out the moment he sensed what that command would be. But it wasn't quick enough.

He felt the burning sensation along the bird's side, and the agony it suffered. The wing had been almost severed by the shot, and its life was swiftly ebbing.

He had to get out of that body and quick ... but there were no more pigeons around except the other nineteen he was already occupying. Nor did any of them have brain capacity enough to contain more than a twentieth of his mind.

Desperately he sent the rest of the flock swirling into the air, seeking other life-forms nearby. There were no other pigeons close enough to hear their calls nor to get there in time if they did, for the wounded bird was dying fast.

Nor were there any dogs about, nor cats, nor animals of any kind to be seen. In desperation Hanlon even tried the trees or plants there, to see if they had minds like the Guddus—but none of them did.

He dreaded to think what would happen if the brain that a portion of his mind was occupying died while in his control. Would that part of his mind then be lost? He had no way of knowing, nor was he anxious to chance it, for he was terribly afraid it would be so. And he certainly had proved he had no mind to spare, he thought in disgust. He had really made a mess of this mission. The only way he could get word to the Corps was through his body, and if he sent his mind back into that now he was a deader duck than he seemed to be. For even that twentieth part could be made to talk.

*Why didn't those pigeons hurry?*

Yet he knew they were searching frantically. This was the weirdest sensation imaginable. People had often expressed the wish they could be in two places at once ...

he was in twenty. And each body was connected with the others by a thin thread of consciousness, yet was thinking and acting independently.

His composite mind almost grinned. If anyone had told him a year ago such a thing was possible, he would have called for the paddy-wagon and rushed that person to the nearest nut-house.

The other parts of his mind were flying all about the enclosed park that was a part of the great palace, searching, desperately seeking some other form of life that could be used as a housing for the dying part of Hanlon's mind.

Suddenly one of them uttered a cry that drew the rest to it on swift pinions, to see attached to one of the trees a huge swarm of Simonidean bees.

"Will the queen do?" the one mind-portion asked anxiously.

There was a convulsive shudder in all the minds, for the birds knew—and Hanlon had heard—how deadly poisonous these native bees were; how they were hunted down and exterminated when found. They were twice the size, and many, many times more vicious and deadly than Terran bees. Even now two gardeners were running toward the tree with a great metal net and flame-throwers.

But Hanlon was desperate. "She will have to do," the aggregate mind decided.

Instantly, then, the part of his mind in the dying bird detached itself and entered the brain of the Queen Bee. There were long, disheartening moments of twisting and struggling to fit into that strange, vicious insect brain. He finally managed to take control, yet was not fully en rapport. Sight through her muti-faceted eyes was very nearly impossible with the little time he could give to learning their texture.

But the close rapport between the various portions of his mind was a good guide. The Queen flew swiftly towards that ventilator, her swarm following closely at her command.

Into and through the vent she flew, and almost before the four men inside were aware of the strange buzzing, she was directing her swarm towards them.

"Bees!" Panek yelled in terror, and the four started fighting the hundreds that swarmed all over each of them.

That may have been their mistake—had Panek and the other two stood perfectly still it was a bare possibility they might have survived, although in Hanlon's grimly determined frame of mind that was now doubtful.

Not that Hanlon was angry, even at Panek for the terrible beating of his unconscious body. For he realized it was the man's cruel, sadistic nature; that he could not have acted otherwise.

But Hanlon knew now that the peace of the Federation demanded that he live and be free to make his report, and only the death of His Highness and the others could now possibly save him.

So, much as it sickened him, Hanlon had to keep on, and as those bee-stings plunged in their hundreds into the four, the poison working far more swiftly than does the venom of Terrestrial bees—more akin to that of the mamba—one after another of the four fell to the floor and were quiet—stung to death.

Hanlon then sent the Queen and her swarm back outside, after first impressing on her mind that she must fly far away if she was to survive. He could not send her to her death by the gardeners after she had saved his life.

As she flew away he recalled his mind back from her and the nineteen birds, into his body. He sat erect once more—but instantly such a tide of pain washed over him that he nearly fainted. For all the agony of that terrible beating hit him at once.

His mind, too, was sluggish and slow once it was back in his own brain where that drug had taken effect. But he felt a sense of satisfaction and gratitude that he had come safely thus far through that terrible ordeal. The drug would wear off, the wounds would heal, and the pain would disappear in time. Meanwhile, he was alive . . . impossible as it seemed, he was *alive!*

But George Hanlon had enough mind-power functioning in spite of the truth-drug, to realize he was not yet out of the pit. His body was still manacled to the chair, that in turn was fastened to the floor so he could not move it.

He was still inside the palace of the conspirators, and it would undoubtedly not be too long before someone would enter the room seeking His Highness, and would find him and the dead men.

For desperate minutes Hanlon considered every angle of the matter, and found only one possibility that might offer some chance of release and safety.

Once more he sent a portion of his mind out through the ventilator and found one of the pigeon-like birds still nearby. Again he took possession and crowded into its tiny brain all of his mind it would hold. Then the bird was swiftly winging its way up and over the roofs of the palace, into the dusky sky.

High in the air it floated on out-spread pinions while he surveyed the city beneath him, hunting for landmarks. He quite easily located the downtown section because its lights were being turned on now that evening was here.

That oriented him, but the fact that it was so late brought dismay. Would the Corps officers have gone home? And if so, how could he locate any of them, tonight, with whom he could possibly communicate? He had not thought of that before—he had been thinking of himself as a man, not as a bird.

But even as these baffling thoughts and questions were plaguing him, he was flying as swiftly as the bird's wings would carry him, directly towards the great building that housed the Corps' contingent here on Simonides.

Actually, it was only minutes until the bird was outside the great structure, and rapidly looking into windows. Lights were blazing in almost every room, and Hanlon's mind knew thankfulness that so many of the high officers were still at work.

Window after window the bird peered through in furious haste, searching for an admiral's office. If it could get inside, Hanlon had thought of several ways in which it might communicate . . . providing the admiral was not an orthodox brass hat.

But, he told himself to maintain courage, any man who could gain as high a position as any of the various types of admirals would have had to show his resourcefulness time and again. You just didn't get that high in the Corps otherwise.

Luck and persistence achieved his ends, for he finally

located the offices of the Planetary Admiral, himself, and that officer and his secretary were still inside at work.

Hanlon made the bird land on the window sill, and then begin tapping with its beak on the glass. Time and again it did this, until the two inside, attracted by the sound, looked about for its source.

"Look, Admiral Hawarden, it's a pigeon, tapping on the window," the secretary laughed.

"Must think there's something to eat in here," the officer grinned back.

"It really acts as though it was trying to attract our attention," the girl commented a few seconds later.

"Hmmm, I wonder," the admiral spoke half aloud, then as the bird kept up its purposeful tapping he recognized the Inter-Stellar code S O S. Quickly he rose, went to the window, opened it, and stepped back.

The bird, showing no fear of the humans, entered and flew to his desk. The secretary had also risen, and now shrank back against the wall, her hand at her mouth stifling a scream.

"It's magic," she said in fright. "No bird ever acted like that."

"It certainly is unusual," he said, and his eyes were puzzled. "I can't make it out."

The bird flew toward the officer, and with fluttering wings poised in the air before him, its beady, bright eyes peering directly into his. Then it flew toward the door. When the admiral made no move to follow, the bird repeated the performance.

"It seems almost as though it wanted me to go somewhere with it," the officer said in a dazed manner. "Are we dreaming this, Thelma?"

"I . . . I don't know, sir. We . . . we must be," she stammered. "It just couldn't be possible otherwise."

But now the bird apparently noticed something else in the room, for it flew over to the secretary's desk and alighted on it. It hopped up to her electro-writer.

That was too much. The girl rushed over, waving her hands. "Shoo!" she scolded. "Get off my desk, you crazy creature!"

But Admiral Hawarden was no fool. This was far beyond any experience he had ever had, but there was such a purposefulness in the bird's actions, strange and unusual though they were, that he felt this little drama should be played out without interruption.

"Leave it alone!" he commanded sharply in a tone that startled her, so different was it from his usual polite manner.

Looking at him in astonishment, she stepped back, and watched with him this unprecedented action.

With its foot Hanlon made the bird throw the little switch that activated the writing mechanism, and then with its beak began pecking at the keys. Luckily there was paper in the machine, a letter she had not finished. The admiral stepped up to where he could see, but waved the girl back when she started to follow. It seemed impossible that the bird could write anything sensible . . . but the admiral was beginning to be not too sure of that.

His eyes opened wide with surprise as he saw the letters appear one by one on the paper:

                    a n d r m a 7

No longer did he doubt. How it was possible, the future might tell. But he did know the significance and the urgency of that message. He ripped the paper from the machine and pocketed it, then jumped to his desk and flipped the intercom switch.

"Captain Jessup! A company of marines, in full armor and all weapons, at the main gate in trucks in two minutes. Hipe!"

He ran to a cabinet in one corner of the room and threw open the door. "Come and help me!" he commanded the astonished girl, dragging his own long-unused space armor out and starting to climb into it. With her help he was completely encased in the minute, and was strapping on his weapons. "You can go home now," he told her.

He turned to the desk where the bird was watching with its beady eyes, and held out his arm curved at the elbow. With a quick swish of wings the pigeon launched itself toward the suited figure and rested on the outstretched wrist.

The admiral plunged through the door and into the hall, where his private elevator waited. "Ground!" he yelled, and the bird was lifted from his wrist by the sudden plunging descent, but fluttered back and rode that wrist as the admiral dashed out of the elevator, through the halls and out the front door to the waiting, marine-filled trucks. Willing hands hauled him aboard the lead truck, and he threw the pigeon into the air.

"Follow that bird!" he commanded, and the incredulous driver did so, wondering secretly if the Old Man had suddenly gone bats.

When he saw beyond doubt the bird's destination, Admiral Hawarden gasped, but he was too old a campaigner to be stopped now. There was something here that needed himself and his men, and he would go through with it, no matter where it led.

He knew the calibre of the men of the Secret Service, and while he could not know how it was possible for one of them to train a bird in such a manner, he knew his job was to back up whatever that high-powered individual was doing.

As the trucks skidded to a halt at the entrance of the Prime Minister's ornate palace, he issued swift commands. His men, disregarding the indignant cries of the palace guards, who swarmed out to stop this unbelievable invasion of their rights, deployed to their designated positions, weapons at the ready.

To the officer of the guard who tried to bar his way, the admiral snapped, "I'll apologize later. Now get out of my way!" Then, with a squad of husky marines at his heels, he followed the fluttering pigeon through the opened door, along a hall, and down some stairs.

But here the bird seemed at a loss, fluttering from door to door, seeking that certain room.

As Hanlon had so shrewdly guessed, Admiral Hawarden was no fool, but quick on the up-take. "Open all these doors!" his voice rang out commandingly.

As fast as doors were opened—whether locked or not made no difference to the marines—the pigeon darted forward and glanced into each one before flying on the next. Then it disappeared through one of the doorways, and the admiral, who had kept as close to it as possible, yelled "Here!" and ran into the room, his men streaming after him.

"Welcome to our cozy nest, Mister," a voice from the depths of a big chair called, and the officer ran forward to where he could see. "You certainly made time, and am I happy to see you soldiers. Get me out of these things," and Hanlon rattled his chains.

At the admiral's gesture the marines made short work of the manacles, and Hanlon stood up, tottered a moment and would have fallen but for the quickly extended friendly arm of the admiral. He was still groggy, even though the serum was wearing off. But he was almost in complete control of his mind.

"We got here in time, then?" anxiously.

"Yes, thanks to my little friend here." Hanlon took the bird, and handed it to one of the marines, meanwhile impressing on its mind that it was safe among friends. "Look after her." And withdrew his mind.

"She gets good care the rest of her life," the admiral ordered the wondering marines. "Wait outside."

Hawarden looked about the room. "Who are these men . . . and what in Snyder's name happened to them?"

"They were stung to death by bees," Hanlon said, and there was a trace of vindictiveness in his voice. "One of 'em's the Prime Minister; the others his gunmen."

"Great John!" the admiral breathed. "This'll raise a stink!"

"There'll be a bigger one before I get through," Hanlon was grim. "Get me back to your office, and get a doctor. They gave me truth serum, and it hasn't all worn off yet. And I'm hungry," he added so plaintively that Hawarden, accustomed enough to sight of death so it didn't affect him too much, laughed.

"What'll we do with the bodies?"

"Guard the Prime Minister's closely. Merely notify the people here where to find the others."

Hawarden called back two of the marines. "Bring that body with us," and they left.

At the entrance the admiral recalled his men. To the palace officer he partially explained. "The Prime Minister was killed, and we're taking his body with us. There are three of his men, also dead, in Room 37-B down there. I'll notify the Emperor, and assume full responsibility."

He jumped into the truck's front seat beside Hanlon and the driver.

"Back to base!"

# Chapter 21

**T**HE DOCTOR, NOTIFIED BY THE TRUCK'S SHORT-wave, was waiting in the admiral's office to give Hanlon the shots of antidote and attend to his wounds. He had barely finished when a waiter brought food.

These two gone, Hawarden felt free to demand of Hanlon, "Open up, please. What's this all about?"

"Full coverage?" Hanlon asked meaningly.

The admiral flipped a couple of toggle switches on his desk. "There is now."

"I'll tell you the story in a bit, but there are several more things to be done, fast."

He described the location of the hidden spacefield. "Get some scouts out there quick, but if the freighter's not ready to leave, have 'em keep hidden and merely watch it. I don't want anything done until just before take-off—it's important we arrest *all* of its crew and passengers."

"Right!" Admiral Hawarden turned to his communicators, and orders rapped out.

"You'll have to tell me procedure here, sir, for I don't know how to get what I need. I want to recommend that the entire Corps fleet rendezvous near here immediately so we can go to a planet called Algon, and take it over. But first we'll have to find out exactly where in space Algon is. May I talk with your planetographers, please?"

The admiral looked at him quizzically. "You haven't been in the SS very long, have you, Hanlon?"

"No," the young man looked up in surprise. "This is my first assignment. Why do you ask?"

"Because in emergencies such as this you give orders, not ask for permission. Every resource of the entire Corps is yours to command when you feel it necessary."

"Why . . . why, I didn't realize that," Hanlon shrank back in astonishment. "You . . . you mean they'd let a pup like me issue commands to the whole Corps?"

"They certainly would, sir. I don't know if you realize

it yet or not, but no one gets into the Secret Service unless the High Command is pretty sure they are exceedingly high-powered individuals. So whatever you want, just yell. I am entirely at your service."

There was a moment of incredulity in the young man's eyes, then he straightened, and that depth of character which the men in command had foreseen came to the surface, and he issued crisp orders. "Very well, sir, I'll take you at your word. Please connect me with the planetographers, then get me the High Admiral."

Hawarden activated the intercom, and when a face appeared on the screen ordered, "Give this young man any information he wants."

"Do you know a planet named 'Algon' or 'Guddu'?" Hanlon asked. "It's about twelve and a quarter light years distant, right ascension about eighteen hours, declination around plus fifteen degrees. Here's a rough chart of what I could see from there." He held up to his screen a sheet on which he had been busily marking such super-giant suns and nebulae as he remembered. ". . . You don't know it? Then find it immediately. Rush it through. I must have its closest approximation inside of two hours!"

He closed that switch and looked up as Admiral Hawarden handed him a microphone. "Grand Fleet High Admiral Ferguson is awaiting your orders, sir."

George Hanlon's young hand was shaking as he took the mike, but his voice was steady and crisp. "Admiral Ferguson, sir, this is George Hanlon of the Secret Service. I was detailed to the Simonidean affair. I've just returned from a planet I know both as 'Algon' and as 'Guddu.' The planetographers are checking now for its exact location.

"The enemy—and I don't yet know entirely who they are, although the Prime Minister of Simonides was one of the top men, if not the actual head—are building a great fleet there. They already have at least thirty-two capital ships in building, and each one of them is about twice the size of our largest battleship. Yes, that's right—twice the size. However, as near as I could find out, none of them are yet far enough completed to fly, and perhaps not even to fight. They also have nearly a hundred medium and light cruisers, and over two hundred smaller ships—scouts, destroyers and so on. Many of those latter two classifications are fully completed and at least partially manned.

"That fleet must be captured or destroyed before they can get it finished. I know you realize that better than I, sir, but it must be taken care of immediately. . . . Oh, no, sir, you can't just blast the planet. There are natives there that are high enough in the cultural scale so the planet cannot be colonized, but they must be freed from the slavery under which they are now held. They are fine, friendly people. . . . You'll rendezvous the fleet immediately? That's fine, sir. Oh, one more thing, please notify SSM Regional Admiral Newton to send all available SS men here at once. There's a lot of cleaning up to do here on Simonides. . . . Thank you, sir, I hope I was in time with this information."

Hanlon broke the connection, then sank back into his chair for minutes, thinking seriously, and the admiral respected his silence. But after a time the smell of that delicious food made Hanlon's hunger and weakness reassert itself. Feeling he had done all he could at the moment, he sat up again, pulled his chair closer to the desk, and lifted the napkin from the tray.

"I'll talk while I eat, if you'll pardon the discourtesy, sir," he began, picking up knife and fork. And as he ate he gave Hawarden as full an account of the situation as he could, except for references to his mental abilities and the part they had played.

The admiral listened attentively, and when Hanlon paused at what seemed the end of his narrative, the officer straightened with determination.

"Then the thing to do now is to find out who all is in back of this. That's why you asked for all available SS men, I understand that. But about His Highness—was he top man?"

Hanlon knit his forehead in concentration. "I . . . don't . . . know," he said slowly. "No one ever spoke of anyone as his superior. He's the man they were all afraid of . . ." He paused a moment, then said, even more slowly, "I've a peculiar hunch. I wish you'd have your best physicians examine that body. Have 'em use X-rays and fluoroscopes, rather than an autopsy. I'm not entirely convinced he was a human being."

"What?" There was incredulity in that question. "What gives you that idea?"

"Sorry, sir, I can't give you my reasons just now," Hanlon's face flushed, and his eyes were appealing. "It isn't that I don't trust you, sir, but there's one secret I feel shouldn't be told now. Maybe later—and if I do tell it to anyone outside of SS men, you will be the first— you deserve that."

"Right, sir. I didn't mean to prowl," the admiral showed no resentment, much to Hanlon's relief. "Your orders go, as I said."

He touched a stud on his desk and when the doctor's face appeared on the screen, gave the necessary orders. "Look carefully to see if the internal arrangement of bones and organs is human—but do not cut without specific orders."

"What about the emperor, sir?" Hanlon asked. "You've undoubtedly formed some sort of opinion about him."

"He was a wonderful soldier and executive as a young and as a middle-aged man," Hawarden said thoughtfully and, Hanlon sensed, sadly. "It was his grandfather who pulled the original coup that made this planet into an empire with himself as first emperor. His son, the second emperor, was also a very good co-ordinator, and solidified the empire status. The present emperor went into the army at sixteen, and rose rapidly through sheer merit rather than because his father was emperor. All historians agree on that. Just bfore he reached thirty he was in full command. He was thirty-six when his father died, and he became the third emperor."

"Then you think he may be back of this whatever-it-is?"

"No," the admiral shook his head. "Somehow I can't quite feel that way. During his first years as emperor he was one of the most cooperative of all Planetary rulers within the Federation."

"What about his Prime Minister . . . and by the way, what was his name? I never heard him called anything but 'His Highness'?"

"His name was Gorth Bohr. He seems to have appeared from nowhere almost overnight—as an important personage, I mean. We've traced him back, and he came to Simonides about fourteen years ago, from Sirius Three.

He's been Prime Minister for about ten years and it has been noticeable that he has gained more and more power during the past few years, as the emperor has been failing both physically and mentally."

"I wonder . . ."

"Yes?"

"D'you suppose that failing health and mind could have been caused, instead of natural?"

The admiral was plainly taken aback. "What? Caused?"

Hanlon nodded. "Just that. From what little I know of His Highness he was just the kind to do a thing like that—and capable of it, too." He sank back in deep thought for some time, as did Hawarden. They were interrupted by a buzzer from the desk. The admiral sat up quickly and switched on the inter-com. "Yes?"

"Bohr certainly was not a human being," the doctor reported, and Hanlon could see the surprise and wonder on his face in the screen. "There are structural differences so far removed from ours that they could not possibly be Homo Sapiens."

"Any idea where he came from?" Hanlon asked, and the admiral relayed the question.

"Never saw anything like it before, and I've just made a quick search through all my books here that contain pictures and diagrams of the races of which we know."

Hanlon shook his head in resignation and Hawarden, after thanking the doctor and giving orders for the disposition of the Prime Minister's body, disconnected.

"Is it too late to get an audience with the emperor?" Hanlon sat erect.

The admiral glanced at his wrist chronom. "Pretty late, but I'll see."

He had just reached for a switch when his call buzzer sounded, and when he activated the screen the planetographer reported, "We can't find any such system on our charts."

Hanlon's spirit sank. "Keep looking!" he ordered. "Check with the astronomers. It's somewhere around there —I just came from that planet. The sun is hot—looks like Sol from inside Venus's orbit, although I don't think it's as large as Sol."

Hawarden then put through his call to the imperial

palace, his position as local head of the I-S C getting him fast service. After some haggling with the emperor's secretary, and his insistence that it was a matter of the utmost importance that could not wait until morning, he was finally told His Majesty would see him.

"Got it," Hawarden rose. "Come along."

Hanlon started toward the door, then looked down at his torn and dirty clothing. "I'm not very presentable."

"We can get you a uniform from the barracks."

Hanlon thought swiftly. "No, I'd better not chance it, although I'd sure like to."

The admiral thought a moment, then stepped back to his desk and pressed a stud. "Roberts, come in here."

A young man almost exactly Hanlon's size, wearing civilian clothes, came into the office. Hawarden grinned. "Those do?"

The SS man smiled back. "Swell."

"Strip," the admiral commanded the astonished clerk. "We need your clothes in a hurry for this man. Quick," as the young man hesitated.

Hanlon was already removing his own. "I'll give you a hundred credits for them, Roberts, but this is prime urgent."

The other laughed then, and started pulling off his suit as fast as he could. "A hundred'll more than buy me a new one—it's a good bargain."

The exchange was quickly made. Hanlon gave the clerk his money, then he and the admiral hurried to the palace, where they were ushered without delay toward the emperor's private study.

"Watch me fairly closely," Hanlon whispered as they were walking down the hall. "If I shake my head, he's lying."

Admiral Hawarden's eyes widened, and though he said nothing, he was thinking, "This is certainly the most amazing young man I've ever met. Where does the SS get 'em?"

They had barely entered the study when a door on the far side of the room opened, and the emperor came in, leaning on the arm of an aide. He sat down heavily behind the ornate desk.

"Well well well," he barked pettishly. "What's all this

about, sir? What's so important you have to get me out of bed?"

"I am most sorry to have put Your Majesty to such inconvenience," Admiral Hawarden said diplomatically, "but you will soon see that this is, indeed, most urgent. It is also very secret, and I respectfully request we be permitted to speak with you alone."

The emperor waved his hand impatiently, and the aide retired from the room.

Admiral Hawarden set a small box on the desk and turned on a switch. "Just a portable spyray block," he apologized.

"I know, I know," came the exasperated voice. "Get on with it, man, I'm tired."

"Permit me to introduce George Hanlon, of the Corps. We have, first, a bit of sad news to give Your Majesty, and then some questions we most urgently request you to answer as fully as you can."

The emperor did not look pleased at this suggestion that he be questioned, but said nothing.

"Your Prime Minister, Gorth Bohr, was killed a few hours ago, Sire."

"What?" The emperor sat upright, his face showing the utmost incredulity, but Hanlon's mind-probing had prepared him for the reaction, so he was not surprised to note neither dismay nor regret.

For the monarch suddenly sank back into his chair, and a long, loud suspiration of relief came from him. He closed his eyes and his face finally relaxed a bit. Suddenly he sat bolt upright. "Are you sure?" he barked.

"Positive," the admiral assured him. "The body is at Base, and has been for several hours."

"How did he die?"

"He was stung to death by bees, Sire," Hanlon answered.

"Bees?" incredulously.

"That's right, Sire. He and three of his men were attacked by a swarm of bees in one of the basement rooms of his palace, and died within minutes."

The emperor was silent for moments, mind roiling. Then he shook his head as though almost not daring to believe this news.

"It may sound strange, Hawarden," he said at last, "but I do not think I was ever as glad of anything in my life as I am of this. He was an evil thing, though I did not even begin to suspect it until years after I appointed him my Minister. By the time I felt sure, it was too late. He had . . . gotten some sort of a hold over me . . . I no longer seemed to have a mind or will of my own any more."

The admiral risked a glance at Hanlon, who nodded agreement.

"Do you know what he was planning, Your Majesty?"

"Planning? Planning? You mean something else beyond ruling Simonides through me, or possibly supplanting me entirely?"

"I'm afraid he was, Sire. Did you know he was secretly building a great war fleet on another planet?"

There was an almost-imperceptible pause before the answer was barked out. "Nonsense, sir. That I can't believe!"

Hanlon shook his head. The emperor was lying now. Why? Was he part—perhaps head—of the plot?

His mind-probing had not yet reached an answer to those important questions. They would have to question him skillfully to make him think of the things Hanlon so desperately needed to know.

# Chapter 22

"THEY CERTAINLY ARE BUILDING A GREAT FLEET Sire, on a planet they call 'Algon'," Hanlon stated crisply, and almost gave a yell of glee as the emperor's mind fleetingly called up a picture—distorted as though it had only been described to him—of one of the Greenies. He hurriedly continued punching. "I know His Highness was the guiding mind behind that, for I was supposed to be working for him, and I've just come back from four months there."

The emperor started to deny it, but Admiral Hawarden stepped closer to the desk and fixed the monarch with a stern eye.

"We don't wish to be discourteous or insolent, Sire, but we know that you do know something about this. Wait, please," he held up his hand as the emperor opened his mouth, so apparently about to demand an apology for the *lese majeste* of calling him a liar. "We do not believe you were doing this of your own accord, nor that you initiated the conspiracy. But we do feel positive you know something about it. And for the peace of the Federation we must have every possible scrap of information you can give us."

The emperor became gradually less antagonistic, and as his face flushed his eyes became pleading.

"I . . . I . . .", he struggled to go on, then realizing that something was holding him back, changed the subject slightly. "I hope, gentlemen, you will forgive me. I don't know what has come over me these past years. I think you know, Harwarden, that I was always heartily in favor of the Federation, and did all I could to make it a force for peace throughout the System. I know only too well how interplanetary war would wreck all our economies, and I do not want that. But I seem to have . . . changed . . . these last years . . . and I didn't want to!" It was almost a sob.

The admiral, as man to man, went quickly around the desk and laid his hand comfortingly on the imperial shoulder. "We all felt that, Sire. You were far too great a ruler to have changed so radically. It puzzled and saddened us all, but now I believe we can begin to see the reason—and it doesn't harm you in our estimation now that we realize you couldn't help it."

The emperor raised puzzled eyes. "What do you mean by that?"

"May I answer that, Sire?" Hanlon stepped forward. "We know now that Gorth Bohr wasn't human— he was an alien from . . ."

"An . . . alien?" the emperor quavered.

"Yes, Sire, definitely. We do not yet know where he came from originally, but we do know he had considerable more—or different—mental powers in some ways, than most humans. You are under some sort of a compulsion or hypnosis that prevents your speaking out. The fact that your health failed and your body deteriorated so rapidly proves it was against your desires."

The emperor was startled by that, and his body shook as with a palsy. He repeated his query, dully, "An alien?"

Hanlon and Hawarden nodded silently. After a moment Hanlon took a deep breath and dared the question: "May we have permission to search Bohr's quarters and offices to see what evidence we can find that will perhaps tell us more about his projects?"

His Majesty straightened with decision, and years seemed to drop from his face and fiugure. "You certainly may. I'll give orders at once, and you can send in as many of your experts as you desire. I can sense the need for speed."

Hanlon bowed his thanks, and the admiral voiced his. "That is very gracious, Sire. The Corps thanks you."

The emperor was gaining strength and his old shrewdness by the moment. "What about that fleet you say is being built on . . . on some other planet?"

Hanlon noticed that hesitation and guessed the reason. But for the moment he let it lie, and answered the question. "It is not yet a serious menace, Sire, but will be shortly if not taken into the Corps' hands."

Admiral Hawarden explained further that the grand fleet was being assembled, and would cope with the problem within days.

"Good. Good. Call on us for whatever assistance we can give."

They talked over many details for some time, then the admiral rose as though to take his leave.

But Hanlon wasn't yet ready. He wanted to pick up that matter he had let lie some minutes ago. He stepped up to the desk and looked straight into the imperial eyes.

"Sire, please think hard with all your will. I believe you know more about Bohr's plans, but that the knowledge was hypnotically sealed in your sub-conscious. Bohr had that power, we know. Please try to break that seal. Bohr is dead now—his compulsion can no longer bind you!"

The emperor seemed doubtful, but at Hanlon's continued, assured insistence, finally agreed to try. He concentrated for long, long, agonizing minutes. Great beads of sweat stood out on his white, strained face, and his hands clenched into tight balls.

Hanlon almost repented, and thought of breaking the spell and telling the suffering ruler it didn't matter that much, that they could get the knowledge elsewhere. But he *had* to have those facts—and if he could suffer as he had done, so could others.

But just then the emperor suddenly relaxed. His features became more composed and natural, and he smiled in relief.

"It is coming now," he wiped his face with his silk kerchief. "Bohr did boast to me that he would one day rule the galaxy. But then he told me I must forget what he said, and I did."

That speech seemed to release him still further from the awful tension that had held him for so many years. He was weary but happy. "He didn't tell me much in detail, as nearly as I can remember. Merely that plans were being made to gain control first of this planet, then the Federation, and after that the whole Galaxy."

"Did he say who was with him in this outrageous undertaking?" Hawarden gasped, and Hanlon added, "We mean, was he alone in it, or was some other planet or system backing him?"

The emperor thought steadily for some time, then shook his head. "I don't seem to remember," he sighed sadly. Nor could he, after half an hour's more concentration. "I am sorry I cannot give you that information, gentlemen. But you will soon, we trust, have reason to believe that we are once more desirous of doing everything possible for the peace and well-being of the Federation."

There were tears in Admiral Hawarden's eyes and he impulsively stepped forward and grasped the emperor's hand.

"Welcome back, Sire," he said sincerely.

Back at Base, there were messages awaiting, that had come in while they were gone. The admiral handed one of them to Hanlon. It was terse, but brought a happy smile to his face.

*"Coming immediately, with full crew. Congratulations. NEWTON."*

Others were from Grand Fleet, regarding the measures being taken for the fleet rendezvous, and the part the Simonidean sector was to play. Another was from the planetographers, giving the spatial location of Algon, with the note that they had finally found it on a star map, and that a survey ship wes being sent there at once.

Hanlon punched a stud. "Stay away from Algon," he rapped out when the scientist's face appeared on the screen. "Don't send that ship until you get permission. Just forget all about even having heard of Algon!"

The elder looked questioningly at the youthful civilian giving him such orders. "I don't know . . ."

"Hawarden speaking," the admiral pushed Hanlon aside and glared into the screen. "That's an order! Forget it, as you were told!"

"Yes, sir. It's forgotten."

Hanlon turned wearily to the admiral. "I'm minus on sleep and strength right now, sir. Think I'll go get some rest. In the morning I'll come back and we'll start searching Bohr's stuff."

"Right, I could use some caulking-off myself. A couple more orders, then I'm going home. Do you want to bunk here at Base?"

"No, guess I'd better go back to the hotel. I can't appear here too much, you know— might be recognized by some Terran officer. And that brings up a problem. What will be my apparent status before the crews doing the searching?"

"Civilian specialist, called in by the Corps," Hawarden was used to quick decisions. "We often use such. I'll sign a pass for you. Better use a disguise and different name, hadn't you?"

Hanlon noded. "False mustache, skin darkened, contact lenses to color my eyes. And I'll call myself Spencer Newton."

Hawarden looked surprised. "You pick a name fast."

The SS man grinned back. "It's the one I was born with,"—and then the admiral really was surprised, but asked no questions. He filled in the pass with that name. "Better come directly into this private office."

When they met in the morning Hawarden complimented Hanlon on his disguise, then quickly reported he had already assembled crews and one was working at the imperial palace and the other at the ex-Prime Minister's own residence.

"Good," Hanlon was well-rested and his voice was crisp. "I think I'll start at Bohr's place."

The two officers left Base, a staff car rushing them to the ministerial residence. They entered and Hawarden led the way down a hall towards Bohr's private office.

But just as they reached the door and were turning to go in, Hanlon suddenly pushed the admiral past it, then jumped across the opening himself. Hawarden turned in puzzlement, but Hanlon signalled quiet and led him into a small reception room adjoining.

"There's one man in there you'll have to get rid of before I can go in," he explained in a swift whisper. "Young junior lieutenant named Dick Trowbridge. He'd recognize me even in this disguise. How'd he ever get here to Sime?"

"Trowbridge? Oh, yes, he was sent here from Terra when we asked Prime for a code-expert."

"Umm, that's right, Dick was a code-specialist," Hanlon nodded. "He was my roomate all through cadet school," he explained. "It would give the whole works away if he saw me here."

"He's our only good decoder," Admiral Hawarden frowned. "We lost our best man. We'll have to use him if any code shows up."

"I realize that, but send him away for now. If we get code we can send it to him at Base."

"Right, sir, I'll fake an excuse."

Some five minutes later Hawarden returned. "All clear now, sir."

They started out, then Hanlon stopped the admiral with a hand on his arm. "Please, sir," his face was flaming, his eyes miserable, but his voice was fairly steady. "Please don't call me 'Sir' all the time. It may be that my position as an SS man carries that distinction, but it makes me nervous. A youngster like me has no business being called 'Sir' by a top brass like you who has worked nearly half a century to achieve the honor."

Admiral Hawarden grinned suddenly, and hugged Hanlon with a fatherly gesture. "You're all right, Son, and I'm for you. From now on you're simply 'Newton'. Anything to make you . . . hey, 'Newton'? Are you . . .?"

Hanlon nodded. "His son."

The admiral's eyes glowed. "Wonderful man, your dad. One of the Corps' greatest."

The young man swallowed hard. "I think so, too."

They had been working nearly a quarter of an hour, sorting through the voluminous papers in the minister's desk and files, when another Corps lieutenant came in, his hand bandaged.

"What happened to you, Patrick?" Hawarden asked in surprise.

"That blasted toogan bit me, and I had to get my hand dressed."

"What toogan?"

"One that must have been Bohr's pet. It was flying all about the room yelling and cussing us out. I was crossing to the corner of the room, there, when it screamed and bulleted over, slashing my hand when I threw it up to protect my face."

Another of the men spoke up. "Took three of us to capture it, and I wanted to wring its neck, but Captain Banister wouldn't let me, so we stuffed it into its cage and sent it to the Zoo."

Hanlon was intensely interested in this, but one thing puzzled him. He signalled Hawarden to one side, and asked in a whisper, "What's a toogan?"

"A native bird here much like your Terran parrots, but with even more beautiful plumage, and they can talk much better than parrots. They seem to have quite a lot of intelligence."

Hanlon was instantly alert. "Get it back here for me."

Puzzled but unquestioning, the admiral went to the visiphone and dialed the zoo. "Admiral Hawarden, Curator. I believe the Prime Minister's toogan was just delivered to you. There was a mistake. Please send it back . . . never mind, sir, what the 'why' is, just return it immediately."

He flipped off the switch impatiently, and looked at the young Secret Serviceman with wondering eyes. A toogan? What on earth did the fellow want with . . . this was the most amazing man he'd ever seen. But he sure did get results.

He turned back to his men. "Anything yet?"

"Nothing but ordinary state papers so far, sir," was the consensus.

"Keep looking. Remember, we especially want any mention of any planets whose names you do not recognize; anything about ship-building, or about mining or other planets."

Hanlon handed Hawarden a note, and the admiral sent a couple of marines off on a run. Half an hour later a truck pulled up in front, and the marines carried in another desk. It was the one from that back room in the Bacchus Tavern.

Hanlon himself went through this, but was quickly disappointed. There wasn't a thing he wanted in any of the drawers. He turned the desk upside down, looking for secret compartments. Finding none, he ordered the marines to take it to pieces. At a nod from the admiral they dismantled the desk.

But it was perfectly innocuous.

Hanlon was just turning away, disgustedly, when a man came from the zoo with the caged toogan. At sight of the familiar room the bird perked up.

"Hey, Boss!" it called out in a clear but whistling sort of voice, "I'm home again." Hanlon had no trouble understanding its words, spoken in Simonidean, of course, but was busy examining its mind. He walked over to the messenger and held out his hand. "I'll take the bird."

The zoo attendant looked at him doubtfully. "It's a vicious thing, sir," he said. "Be careful—it's already injured one man. They say no one but the Prime Minister can handle it."

"It's all right," the admiral spoke. "Thank you for bringing it. That will be all."

Hanlon took the cage and, giving the admiral a meaning look, walked out of the room with it.

# Chapter 23

IN THE NEXT ROOM GEORGE HANLON SANK INTO a comfortable chair, then opened the cage door and the toogan fluttered out and perched on the chair arm. The young man fitted his mind more closely to the bird's brain and began probing. Carefully he studied its every line and channel, utterly oblivious to everything else.

His first brief examination brought a slight sound of pleased surprise to his lips. This bird had a real mind, far better than any he had previously discovered in any animal or bird, even better than a dog's. And he could read everything in it.

Best of all, the toogan had a pictorial type of mind—it remembered in scenes as well as words. It transmitted an almost perfect likeness of the being Hanlon had first known as The Leader and later as His Highness Gorth Bohr—any slight discrepancies being caused by the difference between a bird's ability to see and that of humans.

Like a swiftly unreeling three-dimensional film, Hanlon saw the Minister working at his desk, walking about the room, receiving callers, playing with the bird, eating—and sharing his food with it—talking to it confidentially as he might have done to a well-trusted aide.

For over an hour Hanlon sat there, and the bird, seemingly asleep, sat on the chair arm without making a move. Finally Hanlon rose, and the toogan flew onto his outheld arm much as a falcon might ride. In that manner they returned to the main office where the others were still working.

They were all amazed at this peculiar situation, but only Admiral Hawarden came even close to guessing what was going on. The memory of that astounding performance of the pigeon made him think perhaps this surprising young man had actually been reading the bird's mind—or something equally fantastic.

Hanlon set the toogan down on a corner of the big desk, then started walking toward a corner closet. As he

neared it the bird seemed to come to life. It began screaming, "No need looking there! There's nothing in there.
Nobody's ever to look into that closet! Sic 'em, Pet!"

It dove straight at Hanlon, beak open and screaming
in rage. But the man's hand and mind were quicker.
Taking possession of the bird's mind again, he silenced it
and grabbed it by the neck, holding it gently but firmly
under his arm.

"Open that closet and search it thoroughly," Hawarden
snapped.

Several of the Corpsmen jumped forward, and again the
toogan struggled, but Hanlon was holding it firmly by
force, as well as tightening his mental control, which the
powerful compulsion Bohr had implanted in the bird's
mind had momentarily broken through.

In minutes everything was out of the closet, and while
some of the officers were examining every bit of the contents, others, with powerful, portable glo-lights, were going
over the walls and shelves. There was a three-foot ladder-
stool in the closet, and one of them started to mount it
to search the ceiling.

But the moment the man touched the stool the bird's
mind gave Hanlon a clear picture of a procedure it had
witnessed many times. He gasped, and called out to the
Corpsmen, "That stool! Never mind looking at the closet
itself or that other stuff. Bring the stool out here!"

The surprised lieutenant jumped down, and carried the
little ladder over to where Hanlon was standing with the
bird.

"Unscrew the left rear leg—about the middle, I believe."

The officer up-ended the stool, and after a moment's
work found out how to unscrew the leg—it had a reverse
thread. In a few more instants he had it off, and they all
gasped.

The leg was hollow, and in it were a number of tightly-
rolled sheets of very thin, tough paper.

The Corpsman started to unroll the papers, but at a
quick signal from Hanlon, Admiral Hawarden stepped forward.

"I'll take those, Lieutenant. I think, for the time being,
at least, we need search no further. Since most of the
papers we have found here are purely planetary matters,

they're not for us to meddle with, even though we have permission to do so. Back to Base—if these are not what we want we can start again later."

As the men filed out, Hawarden activated the visiphone, and got the minister's office at the imperial palace. "Find anything we want there, Captain?" he asked the man who answered.

"Not yet, sir."

"Report back to Base, then. I think we've got it here."

He disconnected and handed the papers to Hanlon who had, in the meantime, returned the toogan to its cage, and now sat down. He saw the young man's face fall at first glance at those dozens of rolled sheets.

"What's wrong?"

"It's in code," came the explanation reply as Hanlon swiftly examined each page. "In code—or in Bohr's native language, whatever that may be."

"Ouch! If it's that, we're sunk. Better get Trowbridge on it anyway, hadn't we?"

"Yes," slowly, "that's all we can do now." After some moments, "Guess I'll keep out of sight for a while. I'll go back to the hotel. You can get in touch with me there. I'm still sort of shaky from that beating I got, and need a lot of rest."

"Want the doctor to look you over again?"

"No, I don't think I need that now. He said to have the dressings renewed in two days, so I'll see him tomorrow."

"Right, Newton. If anything comes up, I'll get in touch."

"Oh, be sure and let me know about that freighter. You've had no word yet, I suppose."

"Only that it's still there, being loaded. The scouts are watching it closely, ready to blast at first sign of departure."

"Warn them that we want all of the crew and passengers."

The two started out, but suddenly Admiral Hawarden stopped Hanlon with his hand on the young man's arm. "About that business with the toogan. I'm not prying if you don't want to talk, but shouldn't I warn all the men who saw it, to keep quiet?"

"Shades of Snyder, yes! I got so interested I forgot all

about others seeing me with it. Yes, absolutely, it must never be talked about."

He again looked pleadingly at the admiral. "I . . . I'm sorry, sir . . . but at that I know you're smart enough to have figured out most of it. All right, highly confidential, I can do a bit of mind-reading, and especially with animals and birds, whose minds are not as complex as human's. I can even control 'em to some extent."

The admiral nodded. "I sort of figured as much, with the amazing performance of that pigeon. Your secret is safe with me—it certainly must not be spread around. But I don't mind saying I'm glad it's you has that ability, not me," with a half-hearted laugh.

"It is a load," Hanlon admitted soberly, then brightened, "but it sure saved my neck when Bohr had me prisoner and was about to torture me."

The admiral looked surprised, then shivered. "The bees! I hadn't connected . . .", his voice died away, and after another brief hesitation he left, while Hanlon slowly made his way outside, took a ground-cab, and was driven back to the hotel.

About five the next morning Hanlon was awakened by the stealthy sound of a key in the lock of his hotel room door. His hand slid swiftly under his pillow, and firmly grasped the blaster there.

As he saw the door open and a figure slip inside, in one swift movement he sat up, and switched on the bed light. "Up with those hands!" he commanded the man who was closing the door carefully, his back still towards the bed.

The hands went up, and the man slowly turned.

"Dad!" Hanlon yelled in relief, and climbed out of bed. "How did you get here so soon?"

His father met him halfway, and said from their embrace, "I was on Estrella when your call came. That's only a few lights from here, and they sent a speedster." Then he grinned. "I'm glad to see you're learning to keep your eyes open, even in your sleep."

Hanlon started dressing while they talked. In swift, concise sentences he told his father all that had occurred to him since he started his job.

"Nice work, Spence," his father applauded when he had

finished, then grinned again, "although I ought to spank you for taking such risks, after I told you to take it easy at first. I was a bit worried when you disappeared, until Hooper reported what you were after. But about your job," he continued after a moment, "we had no idea you could get so much. We merely hoped you might find a lead or two for us to work on. But you've practically wrapped this up for us."

"Unh-uh," his son demurred. "It's far from finished. We've got to get to Algon and grab those ships. And if any of them, or enough of them, are in shape to fight, that may take some doing . . . if we can do it at all. Then there's the job of finding out where Bohr came from, and how much of a menace his planet or system or whatever it is, will be."

"Sure, sure, I realize that, Son. But those are incidentals. You've given us the 'what' and 'who' we needed to know. But I see you're dressed, and I'm hungry. Let's go eat."

As they were breakfasting his father asked for details, and Hanlon explained about his new mental powers, and how they had helped him. "I can't do much with men, except to read their surface thoughts," he explained. "But with animals I can do more. I can follow those surface thoughts and memories back and down into their total mind, and can take over and control them. But it won't work with people—humans seem to have a sort of natural block or screen I can't penetrate."

Newton's face was a study as he shook his head. "To think my boy can do things like that!"

"How do you suppose it happens I can, Dad?"

"You didn't get it from me, that's for sure," his father grimaced ruefully. "Perhaps through your mother, from her father. He was a peculiar duck. They used to call him psychic, for he'd get some of the craziest hunches—for lack of a better descriptive word. He often seemed to know a lot of things when no one could figure out how he could have learned them. Say, now that I remember back, he used to have quite a way with animals, too, although I doubt if he had anything like your powers."

"You said I'd probably develop other mental abilities," Hanlon grinned nervously, "but I certainly never imagined anything like this."

"Me neither," ungrammatically. "It's weird!"

They had nearly finished eating when their waiter brought a portable visiphone to the table. "A call for you, Mr. Hanlon," and he plugged the set into a wall-socket.

Hanlon flipped the switch and saw Admiral Hawarden's face smiling from the screen. "We got the freighter just a few minutes ago," he reported. "One of our men daringly mingled with the crew as they were boarding, and jammed the airlock so it couldn't be closed. We arrested them all, with only two of our men injured, and five of the enemy. They're bringing them into Base now."

"Fine work, sir. Admiral Newton is here with me—we'll see you in your off . . . wait, sir . . . Dad says you'd better come here to the hotel. Room 946."

They were barely back in Hanlon's room when Admiral Hawarden knocked. He and Newton were old friends, and greeted each other with genuine warmth.

"That's quite a boy of yours, Newt. He's got the stuff."

"Yeah, I'm sort of proud of him, myself. He's really done a job, especially for first assignment."

"Have either of you any orders for me concerning the mopping up?" Hawarden asked, but looked at Hanlon.

"Ask Dad . . ."

But his father interrupted. "It's your party, Son. Speak up. Right now you're not a youngster just out of school, you are the Inter-Stellar Corps," he added impressively.

Hanlon flushed, but there was a sureness in his voice as he answered, that only the bitter experiences through which he had so recently passed, and which had matured him so greatly, could have brought.

"We've got to liberate Algon and capture those new battleships as quickly as possible, of course. But at the same time we must be trying to find out what planet or system Bohr came from, and take steps to see they can't harm us. That means we've got to exert every effort to get every single person who was working with or for Bohr, and especially to find out if he had any superiors."

"Right. The fleet should be here in another two days, and then Ferguson will want to blast for Algon. The other matter will depend on so many things we don't know yet."

"Has Trowbridge cracked that code yet?"

"He reported first thing this morning that he broke it

late last night. I've assigned several men to help him, and they should have it transcribed soon."

Hanlon turned to his father. "Your men here yet?"

"They're coming in as fast as they can get here."

"Better examine those men from the freighter, and have your gang follow up all leads. They'll have to break down Bohr's hypnosis to get any information. Although," he paused and his face grew thoughtful, "I'm wondering if anyone besides Bohr really knew all he was planning. I'm beginning to believe he was a lone wolf."

Admiral Hawarden nodded in agreement. "I've been forced to the same belief."

Something clicked in Hanlon's mind. "The emperor," he exclaimed. "Maybe we'd better have another go at him. I'll bet his mind's a lot freer from that compulsion now, and perhaps he can remember more of what Bohr sealed away from his conscious memory."

Hawarden nodded. "That's a good bet. I'll arrange it."

Two hours later the emperor was free to receive them, and the four were soon closeted in his study.

"It's a strange, weird feeling, gentlemen," he said when they had explained what they wanted. "It's almost like trying to read some other person's mind. I've felt that Bohr's influence was receding, and I've been trying to see what more I could find."

He sat silent for a moment, then said slowly, almost in a sing-song voice as though reading from a printed page, "I knew he was building some ships on Algon, but I did not know they were warships. He told me they were a new type with an entirely new propulsive principle that one of our scientists had worked out."

"There's always that possibility, of course," Newton said.

"Why did he say they were building them elsewhere than on this planet?" Hawarden asked.

The emperor frowned in concentration, then a peculiar look came over his features. "That's strange," he marvelled. "You would think I would have been sure to ask that, but I cannot find any memory of ever having done so."

"Algon had most of the natural resources for the building of ships," Hanlon ruminated aloud. "There were the mines, the forests, and slave labor to cut down expenses. It was mostly engineers, scientists and special technicians who were there, overseeing."

"I cannot find in my mind the names of any others who might have been in the conspiracy with Bohr," the emperor answered another question. "He brought only one man to see me, with the request that I present him a decoration. It was the scientist who devised the new drive, he said. A Professor Panek, I believe . . ."

"Panek?" Hanlon interrupted. "A heavy-set, ruddy-faced, red-headed man?"

"Yes, that about describes him."

"But Panek was only one of his gunmen," the young SS man was perplexed. "He didn't have brains enough to invent an excuse."

"I wonder, then, what Bohr had in mind to bring such a man here like that?" Hawarden frowned.

"Maybe a trick to help throw His Majesty off guard," Newton suggested.

"Or else just a sop to Panek's vanity, to tie him closer to Bohr," Hanlon said. "A thing like that would have tickled Panek."

"We'll have him rounded up, then."

"No need, Sire," Hanlon explained. "He was one of those men who were torturing me, and was killed by the bees."

The emperor looked at the young man quizzically, and a knowing smile erased much of the tension from his face. "I've heard about that incident. Wasn't it rather peculiar you were not harmed by any of those ferocious bees?"

Hanlon's face was as bland as he could make it. "Not necessarily, Sire. I was sitting still, manacled, you remember. They were moving around and fighting the insects."

The emperor winked, and Hanlon probed into his mind, receiving the distinct impression of friendliness, while the surface thoughts were saying, "I won't pry, but I'd give a lot to know what really did happen—and how."

"The Corps thanks Your Majesty," Admiral Hawarden rose to leave, and Newton and Hanlon did likewise. "We'll keep you closely informed of things as they break," and the three backed from the study, bowing.

# Chapter 24

GRAND FLEET HAD BEEN RAPIDLY ASSEMBLING IN the region near Simonides, just outside visual range, and away from the passenger and freight lanes. Mobilization was now complete.

Admiral Newton and Senior Lieutenant Hanlon had been invited to ride the *Sirius*, High Admiral Ferguson's flagship, and were glad to avail themselves of that privilege. They wore uniforms conforming to their rank, but were disguised so that any chance acquaintances could not recognize them, although there were no other Terrans aboard.

Orders were given, and in strict formation the fleet blasted for Algon. First went the great screen of scouts, fanning out in all directions from a common center, the outer fringes at higher speed until a great bowl-like formation was secured. Then all the scouts standardized their speed. When they reached Algon they would completely englobe the planet just beyond detection range.

Next came the light cruisers, in the same formation, but when they englobed at Algon they would go inside the globe of scouts, nearer the planet's surface. Then the heavy cruisers and battleships would descend in three mass formations, one directly over each of the three known shipyards.

"If any of the ships being built there are in shape to attack—if they have weapons installed and crews to use them," High Admiral Ferguson's orders had been very explicit, "you'll have to burn them down. Otherwise we want those ships untouched."

George Hanlon was thrilled with the excitement of what was coming, yet knew a touch of fear. He had never been under fire, and knew only from hearsay just what it meant to be in a ship that might be destroyed any instant without the least chance of anyone escaping. In space warfare, there usually just were no survivors. You won and lived—or you lost and were blasted out of existence.

But it wouldn't be long now—the scouts were already establishing their globe just outside of detection range. "No signs of being discovered yet," they reported.

Then the light cruisers began slipping through the screen of scouts to take their positions. Suddenly, a number of great beams of energy stabbed up toward them from below, and the screens of the cruisers flared in brilliant corruscations of flame as those mighty rays struck them.

"Don't you cruisers and scouts take foolish chances!" High Admiral Ferguson's voice rasped into the mike. "If those beams are too hot, get back fast! Heavy cruisers and battleships, down!"

Instantly Hanlon could feel the surge of acceleration as the great ship he was riding plummeted planetward. In the plate he and his father were scanning, he could see the dots of blue light that identified the nearest scouts, and a moment later the greens of the light cruisers.

Then those dots fled behind his range of vision as the heavies flashed past them.

The plate Hanlon was using was of limited vision, so he could not see the battle as a whole, as High Admiral Ferguson could in his wide-coverage screens. Only what was going on directly below and close to either side was visible to Hanlon. Yet he could see several of those great, stabbing beams reaching out toward the fleet.

A change in color at one edge of his plate caught his eye, and he saw the ship nearest on his right begin to glow as a heavy beam from below worked on its screens, burrowing its way in and in, trying to blast the ship out of existence.

Great streams of radiance struck and ricochetted from its screens, which were swiftly mounting through the spectrum as more and more power was thrown against them by the enemy below.

The air in the *Sirius* began to grow hotter, and his father answered his inquiring look, "They're attacking us, too, and that's heating us up. Hope our screens hold," he grinned grimly.

"You said it." A shiver of fear gripped the young man, and he could feel himself trembling. His father threw a comforting arm across his shoulders. "First battles are always toughest," he said evenly, and Hanlon calmed instantly.

He turned his attention to the screen again. That neighboring ship was struggling desperately to escape, knowing she could not stand much more.

"What's the matter with that pilot?" Hanlon yelled. "Why don't he flip her over and beat it?"

"Seems to be held by something," his father's anxious voice was tense. "Have those others got some sort of tractor beam?"

"Tractors?" Hanlon looked up in surprise. "I've read about them, but thought they were impossible."

"Impossible to us because we haven't got 'em yet," Newton said absently. "They are theoretically possible."

Every beam from every Corps ship was piercing downward. Suddenly other ships were appearing, and the young man realized that the light cruisers were coming down to add their might to that of the battleships and heavies.

Four of the light cruisers maneuvered swiftly below the battleship next to the *Sirius*, one below the other, and in the instant of their alignment the big ship broke free, while the others flashed away from that restricting, holding tractor, or whatever it was.

It seemed like hours that Hanlon's eyes strained, trying to see what was going on. They had slowed, his spaceman's sense told him, and now he could see they were within the atmosphere, not too high above the ground. Now he could make out huge, squat mechanisms from which those deadly rays were pouring.

The Guddus, with their lack of knowledge of things mechanical, had not reported these to Hanlon, else he could have warned Admiral Ferguson about them, and the attack might possibly have been handled differently.

Suddenly a speaker blared, "Sector Two is in our hands. No total losses. A number of the enemy scouts got away—they're far faster than anything we've got."

A yell rose from every throat there in the control room.

Sector Two, Hanlon knew, was the spaceyard where the scouts and light cruisers were being built. "They probably hadn't armed that field as much as these others," he said to his father.

Newton nodded, then the two walked over to the High

Admiral's station and glanced into his larger bank of plates.

Now Hanlon could see clearly, and at first glance knew that none of the new enemy ships below them were fighting—only those ground batteries which encircled the shipyard. He could see that most of these were now out of action, destroyed by the Federation ships. The others were under terrific bombardment, not only from the ships' beams, but from their bombs and guided missiles as well.

From the looks of the destroyed batteries, Hanlon guessed the explosive bombs had been followed by thermite to complete their destruction.

"We lost many?" Newton asked.

"No totals," Ferguson's voice was gleeful, "except one light cruiser. We must have caught them napping. If they can't put up any more forces, it'll all be over in a couple of minutes."

*A couple of minutes!* Hanlon's thought was a gasp. He glanced at his chronom, and was amazed. He had been sure this battle had lasted for hours—but it was less than ten minutes. It didn't seem possible . . . but he quickly remembered what he had learned in school, and knowing something of those terrific powers unleashed there, the wonder was now that it had lasted that long.

A speaker near them blared. "Admiral Houghton reporting. Sector Three taken. Two of our cruisers blasted, and one battleship crippled. One enemy battleship was fighting us, and had to be destroyed. They've really got something, sir, that we'll want to study and get for ourselves."

Another yell of triumph came from the Corpsmen, and Hanlon felt a thrill of pride in the Service of which he was a part.

Then a moment later Admiral Ferguson called into his mike, "Cease fire, but stand by on careful watch. *Orion* and *Athenia*, send your specialists down in gigs. I'll meet you there."

The landing successfully completed without further activity from the enemy, Ferguson, a number of designated officer-specialists, Newton and Hanlon, some technicians, and a company of marines in full armor, disembarked and marched to the safest part of the ruined, still-burning spaceyard.

Careful examination of the ships there was ordered. The officer-technies, who swarmed aboard the enemy ships, soon began reporting one after another, that none of these partially-built vessels seemed damaged beyond repair.

"Thank heavens they built what few ground-batteries they had well outside the field," Ferguson said to Newton and Hanlon. "We'll get crews in here at once, and complete these ships."

George Hanlon, after his first quick looks about at the damage done, had been sending his mind out and out, trying to get into telepathic communication with any of the natives, but had not had any success. Had they all been killed? Those here at the shipyard, probably yes, he had to admit sadly. The terrific heat would have burned them. But what about the others? Why couldn't he contact them?

"Excuse me, sir," he addressed the High Admiral. "What about the mines and factories?"

"All under control without any trouble, outside of a few individual casualties. Light cruisers and scouts took care of those while the main battle was on."

"I'd like a small cruiser to take me to the mine where I worked," he said, and one was ordered to come down and place itself on special assignment at his disposal.

"Want to come with me, Dad?" he asked.

The two admirals exchanged glances, and Ferguson nodded. "Go ahead if you want to. We won't need you here for now."

In the airlock of the cruiser Hanlon removed the disguising makeup, and it was as his Algonian-known self, dressed in civvies he had brought for that purpose, that he descended at the familiar little spaceport.

His father was intensely interested in that fantastic, seemingly-alive jungle through which they walked to the mine clearing. "I've never seen anything like this," he commented in amazement. "Are these trees and bushes conscious, too?"

"Very slightly," his son told him. "The Guddus call them their 'little cousins,' and I believe can communicate to some extent, but I never could."

As they broke from the jungle's fringe, they saw a double-squad of marines on guard. The two were allowed through the lines, and entered the office. Behind his desk, his face dead white from suspense, sat Peter Philander, and about the room sprawled the engineers, guards and other workers.

"Hi, Mr. Philander!" Hanlon called cheerfully, and at sound of that remembered voice the superintendent's head, as well as those of all the others, snapped up.

"You!" There was incredulity in the super's voice and manner.

"Yep, it's me," Hanlon grinned. "I'm glad nothing happened to any of you."

"*Hmmpff!*" Philander snorted defeatedly. "What's the difference between being killed cleanly in a fight, as against a lifetime in prison, or a firing squad?"

"You'll get neither one," Hanlon said quietly, remembering the power he, as a Secret Service operative, carried. "There'll be a trial, of course, but I know that you, at least, are all okay."

"He's boss, ain't he?" one of the guards growled truculently. "Why should he get off free iffen th' rest of us don't?"

"None of you will be harmed because of your part in the plot His Highness Gorth Bohr was scheming. That is broken, and we know you were all just his tools. All any of you will be tried for are your actions as regards the Greenies. If brutality against them is proven, you'll be properly punished for that alone."

He turned to Philander. "Are the natives all right?"

The man looked up hopelessly, unable to believe Hanlon's statement about himself. "How do I know?" his voice was dispirited. "When the Corps captured us, they dragged us from wherever we were working, and as far as I know left the Greenies untended. They've probably all run back to the woods."

Hanlon looked at his father. "I'm going out to look. I have a feeling . . . ," and he walked out without saying more. Nor was he greatly surprised to see the natives all sitting or standing quietly in their compounds, some feeding from the fertilizer Hanlon was glad to see was still being fed them, others merely resting, waiting.

The gates, of course, were unlocked and wide open, so Hanlon walked quickly back to the hut his crew occupied and stepped inside the doorway. While waiting for his eyes to adjust to the dimness he saw a figure launching itself at him. But as he quickly stepped back outside, in case it was an attack, he saw that it was Geck.

"You came back, you came back!" the native was babbling telepathically in an excess of joy. "When the new humans came and took the old humans prisoners, me said it was your work. Me knew you would come. Me tell other Guddu to wait for you here."

"What about those near the places where the ships were being built?" Hanlon's mind asked anxiously. "I tried to get into contact with them but couldn't."

"Many of they were killed, yet most ran to forests when great fires that destroy were started," was the sad response.

Hanlon was silent a moment, then telepathed again. "There is no need for you all to stay here any longer. Tell all your people to go back to their forests, for they are all free."

Geck turned to the other natives who were crowding close, and Hanlon could see him talking swiftly with that peculiar-looking little triangular-shaped mouth. Soon his mind was suffused with a tremendous wave of joy and ecstasy, and they began dashing out. Hanlon could see them talking to the natives in all the huts, and in moments all the natives except Geck were streaming happily toward the nearby forests.

Hanlon turned to Geck. "I'd like to have you stay with me or where I can reach you for a while. As soon as we can get straightened around, we'll make arrangements to do anything we can for you."

"Me stay with friend An-yon," Geck said simply, and Hanlon was glad and proud of that friendship with this strange alien.

They walked back to the mine office, and there Hanlon told his father about what he had done with the natives.

Admiral Newton was intensely interested, and frankly studied the strange, weird Geck. It was his first sight of these "vegetable" creatures. "Animated trees," Hanlon had first called them, although now they were so familiar to him, and he knew them so well that he thought of them, naturally and without question, as "people."

The young Secret Serviceman explained to the elder about the frequency-transformer he had built—but dismantled before leaving Algon. He suggested that specialists be sent here to see what could be done about teaching the natives any of the things they might want to know.

"But don't let them try to force the Guddus into a mechanical civilization," he pleaded. "Let 'em grow in their own way, and make what progress they can in whatever way comes natural to them."

"Of course," his father agreed quickly. "That's the way we always work with such primitives. We tell them and show them what we have, but only give them what they specifically ask for, whether we think it is what they 'ought to have' or not. Don't worry, your friends will be in good hands. But," there was a peculiar light in his eyes, "I sure would like to watch an autopsy on one of them. A vegetable brain . . ."

"Yes, it would be interesting," Hanlon admitted, "but I'm glad you treat them that way." He turned back to Geck and explained, telepathically, as best he could.

"You stay here with we," the Guddu asked hopefully.

"I'm sorry, but I have other work to do," and then, as he saw how the other lost heart, Hanlon hastened to add, "I have to go help other enslaved peoples on other worlds."

"Then us not try to keep you. But us hope you come to see we many time."

"I'll do that, Geck my friend, every chance I get."

# Chapter 25

"**W**E'VE GOT A PROBLEM HERE," ADMIRAL Newton said as they followed the marines who were taking the mine operatives to the cruiser to be taken back to Simonides for their trials.

"I know it," Hanlon said thoughtfully. "The Guddus are too high in the scale for the planet to be colonized, and too low at present to be admitted to the Federation as true members. Yet they have immense wealth and resources the Federation can use, and something will have to be done to protect them from thieves and others who might again try to enslave them."

"That will never be allowed again. We'll have to make some sort of a treaty with them, probably establish a small base here, and perhaps make some arrangements to mine their ores—if we have anything we can give them in repayment. I imagine you'd better hold yourself in readiness to head the commission that comes to handle that treaty."

"Gee, thanks for that, Dad. They're such swell people when you get to know them. Ordinarily they live like 'children of nature,' in the forests, without need of homes or tools or anything. They feed from the elements in the soil, so there's no food problem. We did give them nitrates here, but that was because they had exhausted the elements in the dirt floors of their prison huts. In the woods that won't be needed. Oh, well, when we get technies here, with transformers, we can find out what to do with them."

"I'm going back to the fleet now," the elder SS man said. "I suppose you want to go back to Simonides to handle the details of the trials of these men. Incidentally, what about this . . . Philander, did you say his name was? Why don't you think he'll need punishment?"

Hanlon explained rapidly, finishing, "So you see, with some psychiatric treatments, I'm sure that inferiority can be cleaned up and then he'll be a real asset to us or whoever hires him." A sudden gleam came into his eyes. "Say, if we make that treaty with the Guddus, he'd be just the man to take charge here, under Corps direction."

"Well, run along and see to it, then. And Spence, did I remember to tell you how proud I am of you?"

Hanlon hugged his father. "Thanks, Dad. I hope you always will be. I suppose the cruiser Commander will let me ride with him?"

Newton smiled fondly. "Not 'let you,' Son. You merely tell him you're going to go along. Admiral Ferguson assigned that ship to you on special duty."

Hanlon's smile was embarrassed. "I still think I'm too much of a kid for so much responsibility."

"Quit looking for sympathy." It was an affectionate growl.

"Okay, then. Safe flights, Dad—see you on Sime soon."

"Yes, I'll probably be there a day or so after you. Safe flights."

Once the cruiser was in space, and the pressure of acceleration abated, Hanlon sent word to the guards to bring Philander to his cabin. When they had done so, he excused them, saying he would be responsible for the safety of their prisoner.

"Sit down, sir," Hanlon said kindly to the wondering man.

"What's this all about, Hanlon?" Philander puzzled. "Who are you, anyway?"

"I was assigned to find out what it was centering on Simonides that seemed inimical to the peace of the Federation. The trail led me to Algon."

"Where you used me to further your schemes, eh?" the tone was bitter.

"Please, Mr. Philander, don't misjudge me until you know all about it. First, let me ask you, did you know who 'His Highness' really was?"

The mining engineer shrugged. "You probably know already, so why ask me? Prime Minister of Simonides, of course . . . but you said 'was'?"

"He's dead now. Did you also know he wasn't human— that he was an alien from some . . ."

"Not human? You're crazy. He was as human as any of us."

"When we get back I'll show you a full-length X-ray of him if you wish. He was planning the conquest of our entire Federation and Galaxy. The Corps experts are still working to find out just what the details of his scheme were, but that much we do know. Did you know about all the warships he was building on Algon?"

"Ships? On Algon?" The surprises were coming too fast for Philander to adjust to them.

"Yes. Did you think your mine was all there was there? We know of nine mines of one kind or another, a number of factories, smelters, and three great shipyards. Incidentally, everything is now in the hands of the Corps."

Philander shook his head in stupefaction. "I'm not calling you a liar, sir, but it's hard to believe you. I knew there were several mines, but not that many, nor about the rest."

"It's all true enough. And I'm still 'George' to you, my good friend, not 'sir'."

That was a little too much for the older man. "What a mess I've made of my life," he groaned.

Hanlon was intensely sorry and sympathetic, but in a way he was glad to see this present mood. It would undoubtedly make easier what he wanted to do. He went over, sat on the arm of Philander's chair and put his arm about the other's shoulder. He gently touched that terrible scar. "When and how did you get this?"

Philander shrank away from him, but the story raced across the surface of his mind, and Hanlon read it.

When he (Philander) was about eight, a gang of boys were playing about an old, tumbled-down building, and somehow knocked out the prop holding up its remains. Three others were hurt, Philander got that cut-scar, and his brother was killed.

"And you've felt all these years you were to blame for his death!" Hanlon exclaimed. "When we get back I'm going to have the best plastic surgeon remove that scar, so it will no longer be a constant reminder. Then a top psychiatrist will give you some therapy, and help you get your mind at rest. After that you'll be ready to take your place in society as a very valuable citizen."

"You forget what's going to happen to me because of my part in this plot," Philander was still bitter and unconvinced.

"Nothing's going to happen to you—you weren't guilty of anything except having been hypnotized by an alien supermentality," Hanlon said convincingly. "I'll see to that, myself."

Philander looked up in surprise. "You mean you . . . a young fellow like you . . . can tell the . . ."

"Not exactly," Hanlon interrupted with a grin. "But this was my assignment, and my recommendations will govern. The main thing is, will you consent to the plan I've suggested?"

Philander sat for long, thoughtful minutes, then looked up piteously. "If you only can do it!"

When the cruiser reached Simonides and Hanlon had seen the other mine workers safely in the Corps prison at Base, and Philander installed in a room next to his at the hotel, he called Admiral Hawarden.

"Congratulations on the mop-up, which I understand was one hundred point oh oh oh percent," the officer said.

"Yes, the other end's under control. How about Bohr's notes?"

"They finished last night. We've got a complete list of all the underlings who knew any of the main parts of the conspiracy, and the SS agents have jugged them all."

"Good work."

"You did a grand job, sir. Again, my congratulations."

"Thanks, Admiral Hawarden. I've got to get busy now, on my report to the Council."

"Call on me for any help I can give. I'd offer you my confidential secretary to dictate them to, if it wasn't so secret."

"Thanks. She would be a big help, but we'd better not."

"How'd you know it was a 'she'?"

"Even a pigeon can admire a shapely shape," Hanlon quipped as he disconnected.

The young SS man was just finishing his report the next day when Admiral Newton walked into his hotel room.

"Gosh, Dad, am I especially glad to see you this time!" his son enthused. "I need you to check this report."

"Let's see what you've got." Newton settled down in a big chair to study the report, while Hanlon fidgetted about the room, anxiously.

"A very clear, concise and complete report, Spence," Newton applauded when he finished reading.

"Where do I send it, and to whom?"

His father looked at him quizzically. "Have you forgotten about the special mail box for SS men?"

The younger man looked astounded. "You mean, even a thing like this merely goes in there?"

Newton nodded. "However, in this case, since I would have been the one to pick it up, I'll take it to Base and transmit it to the Council. Incidentally, future reports should be marked on the envelope 'Report to Federated Council'."

A couple of hours later Admiral Hawarden called Hanlon at the hotel, where he had just finished making arrangements for Philander's operation and treaments.

"Your father and I want you to come to Base at once, sir."

When he arrived in Hawarden's private office, the admiral handed him a pair of silver bars. "These are yours now, Captain Hanlon."

The young man looked up in surprise.

"You were told promotions were swift in the SS—for those who produce," his father chuckled. "The Council was very gratified with your report, and ordered the promotion."

Hanlon looked at the two insignia, and his fingers stroked them almost tenderly.

"You miss the uniform, don't you, Spence?" sympathetically.

Hanlon gulped and nodded silently, very close to tears.

"Are you sorry you made the choice you did—to give all that up?"

A long, poignant moment of silence, then Hanlon threw back his head in a gesture of pride. "No, Dad. I'm honestly glad I did it. To be able to free those fine Guddus from slavery, and to save the Federation from that horrible plot—it was well worth the little suffering it'll cost me. But," and his smile was pathetic, "I do miss the uniform. I was so proud, wearing it."

A moment, then Hawarden spoke. "Here are the transcripts of the Bohr notes," and soon the two SS men were deep in the study of them. When they had finished some time later, they agreed it was a very comprehensive plan.

"But did you notice," Hanlon's eyes were cloudy, "he doesn't say a thing anywhere about the part his planet or system were to play in the conquest?"

"Yes, I'd noticed that." It was a duet from the two others, and Newton added, "For all there is here, you'd almost feel sure he was playing a lone hand."

"If that's true," Hawarden said thankfully, "none of the other men we've picked up matter—we might as well let them go."

"I'd say so," Newton agreed, "if we can prove Bohr was in this for himself, and was controlling them."

"From what I saw of him," Hanlon said seriously after a long moment of thought, "I'd say he was capable of trying it. He certainly had 'the will to power.' And he was no dummy—he had a really powerful mind. But he was cold beneath that suave, soft-seeming exterior. He was utterly without compassion, mercy, or any feeling of justice. He wouldn't care who or what was damaged as long as he could get what he wanted. I doubt if there was anyone he could really call a friend, or to whom he could talk in full confidence."

"Except possibly that bird you told . . ." his father began, absently, when Hanlon interrupted with a whoop.

"Hey, that's it!" He jumped up and ran to the visiphone, and dialed the zoo. "Bring that toogan of Bohr's back to Base!"

"What, again?" the indignant curator asked.

"I'm sorry, sir, but this is probably the last time we'll need it. Please get it here immediately."

"What's the excitement?" Newton asked curiously.

"Your remark reminded me of something I noticed only dimly in its mind, and didn't pursue at the time."

While they were waiting for the bird, Hanlon asked, "What about the new ships? Have the experts got 'em figured out yet?"

"Not entirely. The hulls are about the same as the Snyder ships, only larger. But that new power system is so radically different they're going rapidly nuts trying to understand it. And they *do* have tractor-beams."

No sooner had the messenger left after delivering the toogan than Hanlon had it out of the cage, and perched on the arm of his chair. Then for nearly an hour he sat there, deaf, dumb and blind to all else while he explored every nook and cranny of that avian mind.

"Got it!" he yelled at last, and the bird, freed from control, sprang into the air and flew wildly about, seeking escape.

"What did you learn?" the admirals were as excited as he.

"We've nothing to fear. Bohr was entirely on his own. The people of his planetary system—Canopus—are so far advanced they live on a completely cooperative basis, every one instinctively working for the common good of all. Bohr was an atavism—they caught him trying to 'take over' there, and banished him. He came here, for his restless mind and savage urge to dominate others would not let him rest until he was absolute ruler of some world or system—the bigger the better from his viewpoint."

"And you got all that from a bird?" incredulously.

"Yes. You were right when you said Bohr didn't have a friend except the toogan. I think that's why he sort of liked me—perhaps he felt I would be one. All men have the need to talk to someone, some times, so Bohr chose this toogan, who is really quite intelligent, and who could talk back with him. The bird doesn't 'remember' it all, of course, but it's all engraved on his brain."

"That means, then," Newton said thankfully, "that we won't have to worry about a war with another system or galaxy."

"Yes, and that's a real help," Hawarden added. "Even one man, or entity, like Bohr, could have given us a bad enough time, and perhaps even wrecked the Federation."

"Well, I guess that winds it up except for a lot of detail work," Newton rose. "I've got to get back to my own job on Estrella. Hawarden, call the port and have them ready my ship, please. And it's been good seeing you again. Thanks for everything."

"Safe flights, Newton," and the admiral started calling the spaceport.

"You'll get your orders in a day or two about going back to Algon with the commission," Newton told Hanlon. "Might as well stay here until then."

After affectionate farewells he started out, then stopped, bursting into a laugh.

"What's the gag, Dad?"

"It just came to me that this was once where the son told the father all about 'the birds and the bees'."

"Well," Hanlon quipped, but kept his face straight. "I figured you were old enough now to know."

THE END